A crucial time

"Carol," Jenny began hesitantly, "Carol, would it be possible—I mean, do you think Dad would let me go to Charm School?"

"*What* school?" Carol stopped unpacking groceries and turned to face her sister.

"You know—one of those charm schools they have downtown. They have classes on Saturday mornings for girls my age."

"Oh, heavens, Jenny, those schools are expensive." Carol turned back to her groceries. "Besides, you're charming enough for us right now."

Jenny sighed. Dad would be even less likely to consider the idea seriously.

Not that she really cared about Charm School, Jenny told herself, it was only to be with Dot. The thought that Dot was starting out on something new without her was . . . well, scary. Dot had been her best friend for a very long time, and didn't best friends always do everything together?

BEST
FRIEND

by SHIRLEY SIMON

Illustrated by REISIE LONETTE

AN ARCHWAY PAPERBACK
POCKET BOOKS • NEW YORK

**POCKET BOOKS, a Simon & Schuster division of
GULF & WESTERN CORPORATION
1230 Avenue of the Americas, New York, N.Y. 10020**

Copyright © 1964 by Shirley Simon

Published by arrangement with Lothrop, Lee & Shepard Company, Inc.
Library of Congress Catalog Card Number: 64-14459

ISBN: 0-671-56013-1

First Pocket Books printing February, 1969

15   14   13   12   11   10   9

AN ARCHWAY PAPERBACK and ARCH are trademarks
of Simon & Schuster.

Printed in the U.S.A.

This is for my daughter

Ruth

Contents

Best Friend

Chapter 1

Jenny and Dot

It was the Tuesday before New Year's and the Jason apartment seemed even busier and noisier than usual.

Jenny's ten-year-old brother Andy and his friend Cliff were playing with Andy's turtle, Mr. Ellison. Jenny's sister Carol and her high school friends were practicing cheers in the living room. And little Pauline was hopping from one room to another—to keep her kangaroo company, she said.

In all the commotion Jenny almost didn't hear her friend Dot Jefferson knocking on the door. Then Dot knocked again—their special knock—three slow raps and three fast, and Jenny ran to let her in.

Dot lived in the same apartment building

and had only to run up the stairs to the third floor. What would it be like when Dot moved, Jenny wondered. She was still not used to the idea that the Jeffersons were moving, although she had known for several weeks.

Dot dashed into the room and hugged Jenny.

"Mother's taking some things over to our new apartment and she said to ask you to come along and maybe she'll buy us both hot chocolate in the coffee shop."

"I'll have to tell Mrs. Brooks," Jenny said.

Mrs. Brooks was the latest in a succession of housekeepers who had presided over the Jason household since the death of Jenny's mother three years before.

"Is she still carrying on about that silly imaginary kangaroo?" Dot asked, watching Pauline hop from one foot to another.

"It is not an imaginary kangaroo," Pauline called as she hopped by. "Gladie is a real true kangaroo with purple ears and a green pocket. She is so handsome that the King himself has sent for Gladie.

"And she has a baby kangaroo in her pocket," she added. Pauline was hopping around the dining room table now and was getting short of breath. Her blond hair clung to her forehead in damp wisps and curls.

Jenny smiled. Her little sister, who looked like an angel, had what Dad called an overactive imagination.

"Sometimes I feel sorry for her teacher," Dad once said. "She has that Special Imagination class. Just think, twenty-four imaginations like Pauline's."

It was not really a Special Imagination class. It was a Special Abilities class. Pauline's marks had been very high on some tests, and she was placed in the special class. She really was a very bright little girl, even though Carol and Dad both said that her Special Ability was getting into trouble.

Pauline heard Jenny tell Mrs. Brooks that she was going to the new apartment with Dot. And of course Pauline wanted to go along. Ordinarily Jenny did not mind taking Pauline, but today she wanted to be alone with her best friend. Luckily Jenny's sister Carol overheard the commotion and managed to persuade Pauline that she would have more fun at home. She could be a pretend cheer leader and help Carol and her friends practice cheers.

Mrs. Jefferson and the girls braced themselves against the cold wind and wet snow as they stepped out into the dark winter afternoon. They passed the landlady, Mrs. Cotton, who waved at them as she hurried into the building.

"I wish she'd have our bedrooms painted," Jenny said, her words turning into puffs of steam in the cold air.

Dot pulled her scarf higher around her face. "That's one reason I'm glad we're moving. Wait till you see my *new* bedroom! It's all in white and aqua—and I even have my own bathroom! Everything is new and beautiful in the Essex Arms. I'm going to just love living in an apartment hotel! I know something marvelous is going to happen there. It won't be dull, dull, dull, like the Towers."

Jenny could not see how Dot could think of the Towers Apartments as dull. Jenny thought the Towers was just about the most interesting place to live in the whole city of Cleveland. Three of the six apartments had tower living rooms. The Jasons on the third floor had one of them, and so did the Jeffersons in their smaller apartment on the first floor. The living rooms were high, with a big fireplace and built-in book shelves. But best of all, the front of the room was a real tower—with tall, narrow windows that looked out over the busy street. When she was younger, Jenny used to pretend she was a queen in her tower, surveying her kingdom.

"The movers are coming on Thursday," Mrs. Jefferson was saying, interrupting Jenny's thoughts, "and I don't know how we're going to be ready for them."

"Don't worry, Mother," Dot said gaily. "I'll help."

Thursday! Jenny thought sadly.

Dot and Jenny had been best friends from the day Dot Jefferson had moved into the Towers Apartments two years ago. They had liked each other right from the beginning, and when Dot was not in the Jason apartment, Jenny was downstairs with the Jeffersons. The two girls were even in the same class at school. They were inseparable there, too, and Jenny enjoyed hearing her classmates refer to them as "the two Jays"—Jason and Jefferson.

"Oh, Dot! I wish you weren't moving!"

"But, Jen, it won't be any different—really," Dot replied. "The Essex Arms is only a few blocks away."

At least, Jenny thought, they would still be the "two Jays" in class. And they were in the same Sunday school class at Plymouth Community Church.

"And I can come and visit you, and you can visit me," Dot continued. "It'll be lots more exciting than just going downstairs in the Towers. The Essex Arms has an elevator—and

5

Mother says sometimes we can eat dinner in the hotel dining room."

Jenny shoved her cold hands into the deep pockets of her coat, feeling depressed, but trying to rise to Dot's enthusiasm. But when Dot squeezed her arm, exclaiming, "We're here! Jenny, look at our new apartment building!" all Jenny could say was, "It's very nice, Dot."

"Isn't this marvelous!"

Dot had taken off her shoes and was dancing about on the soft blue carpet in her own room. "I'm so glad you could come with us. I've been dying for you to see everything."

Jenny was still admiring Dot's bedroom furniture when the doorbell sounded.

"Dot, it's for you," Mrs. Jefferson called, and then Jenny heard voices.

"Why don't you go into the bedroom, girls?" Mrs. Jefferson was saying to the visitors. "Dot is in there." And then Jenny saw three strange girls her own age come into the room. The tall girl with long, honey-colored hair was evidently the leader. She walked with assurance a few steps ahead of her companions, and she spoke first.

"I am Edythe Fisher, and these are my friends—Muriel Keeler and Adele Paige."

Jenny noticed that both Muriel and Adele wore their shoulder-length hair in a style similar to Edythe's. Muriel was quite plump and very dark. Adele had chestnut hair and gray eyes.

"We came up to welcome you to the Essex Arms," Edythe said. She looked at Dot and Jenny as if not quite sure which one she should be welcoming. "My mother said a family with a girl my age was moving in, and we thought . . ."

"Oh, thank you," Dot said. "I'm the one who's moving in. I'm Dot Jefferson."

"You'll love it here, Dot," Edythe said. "We have a club . . ."

"And this is my friend, Jenny Jason," Dot added.

Edythe smiled and said very formally, "How do you do," and turned back to Dot.

"I was saying about this club we have . . . It's called the Thursday Club."

"What's that?" Dot wanted to know.

"It's sort of connected with the Charm School. My mother is the director of the school—Brownell School of Charm," Edythe said. "That's downtown. And just this year they started pre-teen classes—for girls eleven and twelve. We three go to classes every Sat-

urday morning. And then Thursday evenings—
seven to eight—we have our club meeting.
That's why we call it the Thursday Club."

"We plan parties and excursions and
things," Adele cut in, "where we can practice
what we learn in Charm School."

"Each girl has her own hatbox," Muriel
said, "and we have club pins."

"What do you do with hatboxes?" Jenny
asked.

8

"We carry our clothes back and forth from class," Edythe told her. "Just like models."

Jenny wondered why they needed special clothes for Charm School, but before she could ask the question, Edythe added, "We do exercises—so we change into slacks or leotards."

"It sounds like fun!" Dot cried.

"Oh, it is," Adele assured her, "and Mrs. Fisher is just marvelous. She shows us how to walk and model clothes."

"If it isn't too expensive," Dot said, "maybe my mother will let me enroll. I have some Christmas money."

Edythe turned to Jenny. "You can come, too," she said. "Anyone can. It's twenty dollars for ten lessons, and a new session starts in January."

Jenny shook her head. Her father had recently said that there would be very little for extras now that they were saving for Carol's college tuition.

"I'm pretty sure I can't."

"I'm going to talk to my mother," Dot said. "I sure hope she'll say I can go."

"I hope so," Edythe said. "But even if she says no, you can join the Thursday Club anyway, Dot. Mother likes to have the girls in the Essex Arms in the club. She says that sooner or later they enroll for the Charm School, and it makes a good feeling here at the apartment— to have all the girls in the Thursday Club."

"Adele was in the Thursday Club for almost three months before she started at the Charm School," Muriel said.

"Why don't you come and see what it's like, Dot?" Edythe suggested. "There's a meeting next week."

"See, Jenny!" Dot said. "I told you something exciting would happen at the Essex Arms!"

Jenny said nothing. Dot did not appear to notice that no invitation to the Thursday Club had been extended to Jenny. Jenny decided to change the subject.

"Do you go to Circle School?" she asked the girls. "I mean, you must be in the other sixth grade."

Edythe answered for the group. "We go to private school—Miss Milton's over on Rose Boulevard. It's a school for girls."

"Dot and I are in the same class. We go to public school," Jenny said, wondering whether this bit of information might not disqualify Dot from the Thursday Charm Club.

But Edythe ignored the remark about public school and was explaining the advantages of the Thursday Charm Club when Mrs.

Jefferson announced that she was ready to leave.

"I promised you girls hot chocolate," she said. "Perhaps your new friends would like to join us."

Jenny hoped they would say no, but Edythe accepted for the three.

Jenny pulled Dot to one side as they led the group down the hall to the elevator. "Why do they have to come? I'm kind of tired of hearing about their club and their Miss Milton on Rose Boulevard. Or is it Miss Rose on Milton Boulevard?"

"Sshh," Dot said. "They'll hear you."

Jenny felt an unreasoning anger at Dot. What if they did hear?

The hot chocolate came—topped with thick whipped cream. This was a favorite of Jenny's, but today it did not taste good at all. She was glad when they had finished and it was time to leave the restaurant and the Essex Arms.

On the way home Jenny began thinking about New Year's Eve and her thoughts cheered her up considerably. The Jasons always had an open house kind of party on the last night of the old year. Last year Jenny and Dot had made fudge, and Dot had stayed all night at the Jasons'. On New Year's Day the

two girls had helped Carol prepare brunch—
and later went ice skating at Forest Hills
Park.

"I can hardly wait until New Year's Eve,"
Jenny said to Dot. "Carol's friends are coming
this year—and Marge from the Answering Service. I'll bet we can make fudge again."

"That would be fun," Dot agreed.

They had reached the Towers Apartments
now, and Jenny said to Dot's mother, "May
Dot sleep at my house New Year's Eve? Like
last year?"

Mrs. Jefferson smiled. "I've been so busy I
hadn't even thought about New Year's," she
said. "We'll have to see."

Before Jenny could say anything further the
door to the apartment building opened, and
the thick form of Mrs. Brooks pushed past
them. The housekeeper was wearing her green
coat, and she carried two bulky suitcases. She
looked neither to the right nor left, and handed
her suitcases to a taxi driver who had stepped
out to take them.

"Isn't . . . wasn't that your housekeeper?"
Mrs. Jefferson asked.

"Yes," Jenny said, "that was Mrs. Brooks.
I—I'd better run in and find out what happened."

As Jenny walked upstairs she had to

squeeze past Mrs. Cotton, who was coming down.

"Looks like your housekeeper is gone for good," the landlady observed cheerfully.

"I don't think so, Mrs. Cotton," Jenny answered. "She's probably just going on an overnight visit—or something."

But even as she raced up the stairs, Jenny knew that Mrs. Cotton was right. For one reason or another Mrs. Brooks had made an unexpected and hasty exit, and the Jason family was "between housekeepers" again.

And this always meant trouble. The last time they were between housekeepers—some five months ago—Carol had been compelled to stay home from school for four days, because Pauline was sick and could not be left alone.

The door to their apartment was open, and Jenny, stepping inside, saw that her father was home.

Chapter 2

Edythe

If Dad was home in the middle of the day, this *was* a crisis. Jenny saw that the entire family was assembled in the living room and the company had gone.

This had all the earmarks of a family conference.

"Hi, there, Jen," Dad called out, with what seemed to Jenny to be false heartiness.

He was sitting in the wing chair by the fireplace. He was a big man, but very thin. Tall and lanky was the way most people described Howard Jason. And he had a wide smile that always made Jenny feel good. But he was not smiling now.

"What—what's wrong?" Jenny asked.

"Nothing's wrong," Andy said. "Grandma Jason is coming to live with us!"

Jenny blinked. Grandma Jason was Dad's mother, but Grandma lived in southern France, and it was ten years since she had been in the States. Jenny couldn't remember her at all.

"Grandma writes that her project is just about completed," Dad said, and Jenny nodded. Grandma's "project" was the Christine Stengle Home for War Orphans.

"She's coming week after next," Andy said. "And she's going to stay with us, and we won't need any more housekeepers."

"What happened to Mrs. Brooks?"

Andy looked guilty. "That was my fault," he said. "When the letter came I called Dad at the office, and he said to read it to him over the phone, and I did, and I said, 'Hurray, Grandma's coming!' "

"And the next thing we knew Mrs. Brooks was saying she wouldn't work in a household where there was another woman and nobody was going to move in here and order *her* around," Carol supplied. "So by the time we called Dad again and he got back here, she had all her things packed."

"I guess she thought Dad would beg her to stay," Andy added, "but he didn't."

"I think we can take care of ourselves for a

while," Dad said, "at least until Grandma comes." But he looked worried.

The children, all talking at once, assured him that they could manage. Jenny knew that her father was very proud of his children and their ability to pitch in and keep things going.

"It'll be fun this time," Jenny said. "Because now we know there won't be any more housekeepers. We can keep saying, 'Grandma is coming to take care of us in two more weeks.'"

"Jenny, for goodness sake, take your boots off," Carol said. "They're dripping all over everything."

Jenny unzipped her boots and took them off. But before carrying boots and coat out to the front closet, she slid over to the chair and gave her father a hug.

"I'm so glad Grandma is coming," she told him.

"'Jenny kissed me when me met,'" Dad recited, "'jumping from the chair she sat in...'"

Jenny smiled to herself as she hung her coat in the closet. She always loved to hear her father quote that poem. It made her feel very special—almost like Leigh Hunt's "Jenny,"

who was Jane Carlyle. Jenny said the poem to herself:

"Jenny kissed me when me met,
     Jumping from the chair she sat in.
Time, you thief, who love to get
     Sweets into your list, put that in:
Say I'm weary, say I'm sad,
     Say health and wealth have missed
          me,
     Say I'm growing old, but add,
          Jenny kissed me."

However, things didn't seem so fine the next morning. Jenny, who had planned to go to the new apartment with Dot, had to stay home with the younger children while Carol shopped.

"I'll be over right after lunch," Jenny promised Dot. "And I can help you put things away and we can really talk."

But it was nearly three o'clock before Jenny could leave. When Carol returned from shopping there was lunch to prepare and groceries to put away. Then Carol went downstairs to put clothes in the washer while Jenny dried the lunch dishes.

And then, just as Jenny put on her coat,

Carol remembered some things she needed from the drugstore.

"But Sherman Drug is in the opposite direction," Jenny protested, "and I'm late as it is."

"There'll still be plenty to do when you get there," Carol said. "I'll bet Dot is thrilled with her new bedroom."

"She sure is. And not only that, she says it's going to be so much more exciting than living in the Towers," Jenny answered.

This reminded Jenny of something else. "Carol," she began hesitantly. "Carol, would it be possible—I mean, do you think Dad would let me go to Charm School?"

"*What* school?" Carol stopped unpacking groceries and turned to face her sister.

"You know—one of those charm schools they have downtown. They have classes on Saturday mornings for girls my age."

"Oh, heavens, Jenny, those schools are expensive." Carol turned back to her groceries. "Besides, you're charming enough for us right now."

Jenny sighed. Dad would be even less likely to consider the idea seriously.

Not that she really cared about Charm School, Jenny told herself, it was only to be with Dot. The thought that Dot was starting

out on something new without her was . . .
well, scary. Dot had been her best friend for a
very long time, and didn't best friends always
do everything together?

"Don't daydream, Jen," Carol was saying.
"The sooner you get to the drugstore, the sooner you can go to Dot's new apartment."

Sherman Drugstore was in the Sherman
Building. The entire first floor of the building
was given over to shops and stores. There was
a florist shop and a hat shop and the drugstore. A dress shop had just moved out, leaving a big empty double store with gaping
windows.

Most interesting of all was a Chinese restaurant. Jenny had been there once with Dad,
and now every time she walked by, Jenny
thought she could smell the steamy, good
soup.

On the second and third floors of the Sherman Building were offices. Dad's accounting
office was on the second floor—and just two
doors down the hall was the Service. The
Service was really Marge's Telephone Answering Service. There was a big room filled with
switchboards, and in some mysterious way
Dad's office telephone was hooked up to
Marge's boards, so that she or her operators

could answer Dad's telephone when he was away from his office.

Sometimes Jenny went into the switchboard room for one reason or another, and she always watched in rapt amazement as Marge and the other operators pulled cords and turned keys. "Gert's Beauty Parlor," they'd say, "good morning." Or, "This is Dr. Brown's office."

Now Jenny saw that the empty store had been rented. Some men were bringing in long green steel shelves, and someone was pushing a desk toward the front window. A woman with red hair stood near the window, showing where she wanted the desk. There were several plants on a chair, and a telephone on the floor.

As she walked past the almost-empty store and into the drugstore, Jenny wondered what kind of business *this* was going to be.

Jenny arrived at the Essex Arms Apartment Hotel out of breath and tired. No doubt Dot had been wondering where she was—or perhaps Dot thought she was not coming at all. Jenny always worried about what people were thinking when she was late. She pressed the button marked 6, and the elevator rose slowly.

Jenny rapped on the door to the Jefferson apartment three times before there was an answer. Then the door opened slowly, and a voice said coolly, "Oh, hello." It took Jenny a moment to realize that the voice belonged to Edythe.

"Is . . . isn't Dot here?"

"Yes, but she is very busy," Edythe answered. "I don't really think Dot wants company today."

"But I'm not company," Jenny said, hurt by Edythe's rudeness and even more hurt because this girl made her feel like an intruder.

"I'm not company," she repeated. "I came to help Dot, and she is expecting me."

"She doesn't need any help," Edythe said.

"But Dot *asked* me to come . . ." Jenny began, and then stopped.

Oh, *why* did she have to make explanations to Edythe? Why didn't Dot come to the door herself?

"Dot!" Jenny called. "Dot, come here!"

"*I've* been helping Dot," Edythe said, but Jenny ignored this information.

"Let me in, for heaven's sake, *will* you!" she said crossly and shoved against the door. Edythe stepped backward at the same moment that Dot appeared in the living room.

"Well, you don't have to knock me over!" Edythe said, and then she turned to Dot. "I tried to tell her that you're busy and that . . ."

"Oh, hi, Jen," Dot said. "I was just washing out some things and was all sudsy. Come on in."

She was already in, Jenny told herself, no thanks to either of them. But she followed silently to Dot's bedroom.

"I'm glad this apartment was partly furnished," Dot said. "My room was practically in order by the time we got here today."

"The Essex Arms has elegant things," Edythe put in. "Your bedroom furniture is just beautiful. Say, where should I put these jars?"

Edythe and Jenny ignored each other, while Dot talked to both of them, apparently unaware of the tension.

"This would be good for New Year's Eve," Edythe said as she shook out Dot's best dress and hung it in the closet. "The Thursday Club is having a New Year's Eve party. It's going to be at my apartment."

"Dot is coming to my house for New Year's." The words rushed out before Jenny could stop them. "My family always has a party and Dot always comes. She's probably going to stay all night—like last year."

24

Edythe had turned toward the closet again, and Dot was very busy refolding a sweater.

"Mother didn't say I could," Dot began slowly.

"She said she'd think about it, and she'll let you if you say you really want to."

"As a matter of fact," Dot continued, "Mother would like me to stick close to home this year. Since we've just moved and everything. . . She thought a party right here in the building was a good idea."

Jenny tried to control her voice. "You mean you'd rather go to Edythe's party than come to my house!"

"Maybe you could come, too," Dot said quickly. "Edythe, do you think Jenny could come?"

"Oh, no!" Edythe seemed shocked at the idea. "This is only for Thursday Club members. And to be a member . . ."

"I know!" Jenny cut in. "To be a member of your great, superior club you have to go to Charm School—or else you have to live in the Essex Arms. Well, you can both have your miserable old club. And you, Dot Jefferson, you can have your snooty old friend Edythe!"

Jenny turned and ran out of the bedroom.

When she left the apartment Jenny

slammed the front door behind her, announcing her departure. But although she waited in the hall for several minutes, there was no sign of Dot. Finally Jenny pressed the button for the elevator.

At home Jenny's unhappiness went almost unnoticed in the preparations for dinner and the excited talk of Grandma's coming. It wasn't until Jenny and Carol were alone in the kitchen, finishing the dinner dishes, that Carol asked, "Is something wrong, Jen? You've been so quiet."

"No, not really," Jenny answered. She didn't want to talk about what had happened—not just now anyway.

"You were your old bright, cheerful self when you left to visit your friend Dot."

It was the word friend that did it.

"She's *not* my friend!" Jenny cried out. She threw her dishtowel down on the table and ducked past Carol. The tears she had held back since the argument with Dot spilled over at last, and by the time Jenny reached the bedroom she shared with Pauline she couldn't control her sobbing.

"She's not my friend!" Jenny kept repeating over and over. "She's not my friend!"

Carol followed her. "Don't you want to tell

me about it?" she asked. "Sometimes you feel better after you've told someone."

Telling the story to Carol took a bit of the sting out of the afternoon, and eased the tightness in Jenny's throat and chest.

"And the worst of it is that Thursday Club, Carol. Edythe is practically *luring* Dot away with that old club and the hatboxes and club pins."

"That is pretty mean," Carol agreed. "How do you get into this club?"

"You have to be enrolled at the Charm School—Brownell, I think she said it was. Anyway, Edythe's mother is the director. Or else if you live at the Essex Arms, she lets you join the club anyway."

"So that's why you asked if you could go to Charm School," Carol said.

"That would be one way to join the club. Edythe couldn't keep me out if I went to the Charm School."

"That's an expensive way to get into a club," Carol told her.

"Edythe said the school charges twenty dollars for ten lessons. And there are three ten-lesson sessions a year."

"And what do they teach in this Charm School for sixty dollars a year?"

"Edythe says they do exercises and learn how to select clothes and take care of their skin and hair. And she says they learn etiquette and basic poise."

Carol smiled. "From what you tell me about Edythe, she'd be better off learning about basic kindness."

"But, Carol . . ." Jenny wanted to go back to the subject of Charm School. "It does sound exciting—the hatboxes and all. And Edythe says that some of the girls are chosen to model sometimes. Her mother says the graduates will have a good chance to get on the Teen Boards of the department stores."

"Well, you know I was runner-up for that last year," Carol said. "Our school was asked to choose girls for Higbee's Teen Board, and I was the one picked from my class. But Higbee's chose the twelfth grade girl."

"Weren't you terribly disappointed?" Jenny asked.

"Not really," her sister told her. "There are so many interesting things to do when you are in high school. I guess if I were interested in merchandising I would have tried again this year. But I'm interested in journalism, so I spend my time working on the paper."

"You have so many special activities, Carol," Jenny said. "And so many friends."

Carol looked troubled. "Jenny," she said, "don't you think it would be better if *you* had ... well, more friends? Then you wouldn't be so dependent on Dot."

Jenny sighed. It was easy for Carol to tell her to have more friends. Carol still had her best friend, Bunny Monroe. Carol wasn't without a best friend.

"I don't care about lots of friends," Jenny said. "I just want my best friend back. There's nothing like a best friend."

"Of course, there's nothing like a best

friend," her sister answered, "even if they do create problems at times. Hey, Jen, let's talk about the New Year's party. You can help me plan the menu."

Jenny found herself enjoying New Year's Eve in spite of Dot's absence. The Jason apartment was crowded with guests—her father's friends, Carol's friends, and even Andy's pal, Cliff Clark. All the children—even little Pauline—were allowed to stay up to see the New Year in. There were songs and games and some square dancing—until the people downstairs tapped on the ceiling. That night Jenny went to sleep tired and less unhappy than she had been the day before.

The Jasons were just finishing a late brunch on New Year's Day when the front doorbell rang. Carol, who had gone to press the buzzer and open the door, came back to the dining room and announced, "Dot's here, Jenny."

Chapter 3

Ruthie

Dot was standing in the center of the foyer, twisting her brown gloves around and around.

"Well . . . well, hi, Dot. For heaven's sake, come on in!" Jenny started to lead the way into the living room, but Dot hung back.

"I just came to tell you Happy New Year," Dot began.

"Happy New Year!" Jenny answered.

"Happy New Year," Dot said again, and suddenly Jenny giggled.

"What's so funny?" Dot asked.

"You," Jenny told her. "Us. You come over here and stand right there as if—as if you've taken root, or something. Come on in and have milk and French toast with us. You don't have to act like company, Dot—or a stranger or something—just because of that argument."

"That's really what I came about," Dot said. "I didn't want to start the New Year mad at you."

"Neither did I," Jenny said. Then she added, "How was the party?"

"Okay, I guess. But I missed you. How was your party?"

"It was great, but I missed you, too."

Suddenly Jenny felt very good. "Keep me company while I help Carol clean up, then we can do something."

"Ice skating," Dot said. "I was thinking about it on the way."

"Ice skating," Jenny agreed, and the two friends went into the dining room arm in arm.

The glance that Carol flashed Jenny was a question, but when Jenny grinned and announced that she and Dot were going ice skating, Carol offered to do the dishes herself. "Just help me clear the table."

Dot did not want anything to eat. She had just had brunch at home, she said. As Jenny stacked the plates and saucers in the kitchen, she heard Andy talking to Dot.

"I hear you moved into my friend Cliff Clark's house."

Jenny smiled. Andy made it sound as if Cliff Clark owned the Essex Arms Apartments.

Dot spoke glowingly about the Essex Arms, and then Andy asked her to play chess with him. He was already setting up the board.

"Don't do it, Dot," Jenny called. "It might take forever, and I'll be ready to leave in a few minutes."

"Forever—nothing!" Andy said. "I can beat her hollow in ten minutes."

Dad laughed. "Is that supposed to be an inducement?"

"Unfortunately, it's true," Dot said. "Andy can chase me off the board before I've barely started. No, thanks."

"Aw gee," Andy sounded hurt. "Nobody wants to play with me. Say, Carol, what about you?"

"Not me," Carol answered quickly. "You beat me yesterday and twice the day before. Nobody likes to lose *every* time."

"Trouble with me is I'm too good," Andy said sadly, and Jenny had to smile. It was true. Andy's teacher called him a "mathematical wizard," and it was probably this that made him so good at chess. He could visualize moves that were three plays away.

"I'll play with you, Andy," Pauline offered. "Soon's I tie Gladie up in the basement."

But Andy was not interested in playing chess with Pauline. She made up her own rules.

The telephone rang and Pauline dashed off to answer it. She always wanted to answer the telephone, to the annoyance of the others. One never knew what Pauline would say. Sometimes she told complete strangers about Gladie.

This call was for Dad.

"It's the Service," Pauline said. "They said there's a message from Christopher Columbus."

Carol laughed. "It's probably from Columbus, Ohio," she said. "Dad has a client there."

The girls were ready to leave now, and Jenny took her own skates and borrowed Carol's skates for Dot.

"It's a good thing you wear the same size and don't have to go home to get yours," Jenny commented.

The truth of the matter was, Jenny admitted to herself, that she would hate to stop at the Essex Arms for Dot's skates and run into Edythe.

All of the skaters in Cleveland Heights seemed to be descending on Forest Hills Park this morning, and Jenny was glad that the lake was a big one. The girls skated around and around the lake, occasionally stopping to call to a classmate or friend. Sometimes they skated separately, sometimes arm in arm. It was just like the times before Dot had moved to the Essex Arms, Jenny told herself, and she felt glad all over—glad for the crisp winter day, the frozen lake, the skaters, but most especially glad to be with her best friend.

After skating the girls sat sipping their chocolate in a little restaurant near the Park. Jenny was sorry to see vacation come to an end, but Dot was looking forward to Tuesday and school. "I'm anxious to know what part I'm going to get," she said.

Jenny remembered that parts would be given out for the *Alice in Wonderland* marionette play next week. This was Miss Blake's class project for the year. Their sixth grade had finished reading *Alice* a week before vacation and were making plans for the play. Each pupil had submitted a sketch of the character he or she wanted to portray, and Dot hoped to get an okay on Alice. This meant making the marionette and later playing the part. Jenny herself had submitted two sketches—one of

Alice and one of the Queen of Hearts. But
Jenny had little hope of playing the lead. As a
matter of fact, she didn't really want the part
of Alice if Dot was so set on it.

On the way home the girls decided to celebrate the last day of vacation, on Monday, by
a special excursion: a visit to the Art Museum,

lunch at the Museum cafeteria, and perhaps skating in the afternoon.

Jenny, who planned to get up very early on Monday, was surprised to see the sunlight filling her room when she opened her eyes. The family was already at breakfast, and Dad was ready to leave for the airport. He had to spend the day in Columbus, he said. When Carol announced that she intended to attend church choir rehearsal at eleven, Jenny looked up.

"But Dot and I are going to the Art Museum," she began. "Well, Andy will watch Pauline."

Her brother pushed a stubborn strand of brown hair away from his forehead and informed her that he and Cliff Clark had a date to walk two Dalmatians belonging to Cliff's aunt. This was, after all, a *job*.

"You can take Pauline with you, Jenny," Andy said.

Jenny said nothing, but Pauline, sensing that Jenny was displeased, volunteered to tie Gladie to the bedpost. At least, Jenny thought, her sister wouldn't be stopping to talk to the imaginary kangaroo.

But Pauline's presence was the least of her troubles, Jenny was to find out when they reached the Essex Arms. Dot was downstairs, waiting for her. She looked troubled.

"Say, Jen," Dot began. "Don't be angry, but . . .Well, Edythe came over this morning and she asked what I was doing today, and I said . . . I said you and I were going to the Art Museum. And she said she was all alone."

Jenny felt a wave of bitter disappointment. She knew what was coming.

"Anyway . . ." Dot seemed to have difficulty continuing. "Anyway, she asked if she couldn't *please* come along, and well . . ."

"You said yes."

"Well, what else could I say? Gee, Jen, don't be mad. Edythe will be here in a minute. She had to get something for her mother. You're not mad or anything?"

Jenny wanted to shout that she was *very* mad, that she had been looking forward to this day alone with her best friend. But before she could figure out a way to say what she felt without sounding mean and selfish, Edythe appeared. Edythe had her skates over her shoulder. Dot, Jenny saw, also had her skates.

"Hi!" Edythe called. "Oh, I see we've got other company," she said, looking Pauline up and down.

"Guess what, Dotty? My mother says you can have dinner with us—downstairs in the dining room. And then we'll all go to the movies. Or we could watch color television in our apartment."

Dot's eyes shone. "Oh, Edythe," she said, "that would be great!"

Edythe chattered all during the bus ride,

ignoring Jenny and Pauline. She talked about the Charm School, of course, and Jenny learned that Dot was planning to use her Christmas money to pay part of the tuition.

"Does your mother really want you to go, Dot?" Jenny asked, remembering Carol's reaction to the school.

"At first she said no," Dot told her. "But then I told her how much I want to go. So she said I could try it for the first ten weeks."

The girls had a two-block walk from the bus. Once again Edythe did most of the talking. "My mother says I'm very lucky that you moved in just when I really *need* a new best friend." Edythe linked arms with Dot and pulled her a few steps ahead, forcing Jenny to walk behind them with Pauline.

The situation was not improved by Pauline's spilling milk all over her skirt at the Museum cafeteria.

"It's all Gladie's fault," Pauline said in a high, clear voice as Jenny tried to mop up her sister's dress with a napkin. "She must have untied herself from the bedpost and hopped right over here and bumped into my elbow and made me spill my milk."

"Who is Gladie?" Edythe asked.

Dot giggled. "You mean *what* is Gladie?"

Jenny decided suddenly that she would take Pauline home and leave her there. Andy or Carol should be home by now, and one of them could watch Pauline for the rest of the afternoon.

"Hey, look at my loose tooth," Pauline announced. "It's hanging by a thread!"

"Ugh!" said Edythe.

"We have to go," Jenny said as she prodded her reluctant sister.

"You will come back, won't you?" Dot asked.

"I don't know," Jenny answered. "The bus ride takes at least ten minutes. And sometimes you have to wait quite a while for a bus."

"And there's a walk to the bus," Edythe said.

Edythe needn't be so anxious to get rid of her, Jenny thought.

"As a matter of fact, the whole trip will take you too long," Edythe said. "I've seen as much of the museum as I want to. We might as well go skating."

Jenny felt herself getting very angry. She and Dot had planned to stay as long as they wanted at the museum, and they hadn't seen half the exhibits. Without a word Jenny took Pauline's hand and walked away.

"Jenny!" Dot called, and Jenny turned.

"Jenny, why don't you meet us at the lake? You could take Pauline home and pick up your skates." Jenny said she would see.

On the way home Jenny decided that she would not join Dot and Edythe at the lake. She had had just about enough of Edythe. And she was very annoyed with Dot Jefferson. Dot should have said something when Edythe made that remark about needing a "new best friend." Dot could have said, "I already have a best friend," or "Jenny and I have been best friends for years." *I am the one who should look for a new best friend,* Jenny told herself.

Yes, that was what she would do—look for a new best friend.

Jenny was disappointed to find that neither Andy nor Carol was at home. She was just taking off her coat when the telephone rang.

It was the Answering Service. Would she ask Dad to call as soon as he returned home. There were several messages.

"Is that you, Jenny? This is Marge. You don't sound like yourself."

"It's me. . . I mean I. This is Jenny."

"Well, gee whiz, Jenny. You sound as if you had just lost your last friend."

"I lost my *best* friend," Jenny said. She felt worse than ever.

Marge clicked her tongue. "Come on over here, Jenny honey," she said. "I'll let you work the switchboard a little. That should cheer you up."

When she was a very little girl, Marge sometimes allowed her to "work the switchboard." "Plug in there, honey," Marge would say, guiding Jenny's hand. Marge obviously didn't realize that Jenny was no longer a little girl. But it was nice to have someone sympathize with her.

"Thanks, Marge," Jenny said. "But I have to watch Pauline."

"Bring Pauline along. My little daughter will be here soon. Her grandmother brought her down on a shopping trip, and they're going to stop here on the way home."

Anything was better than staying in the apartment and hearing about Gladie, Jenny told herself as she started out with the freshly dressed Pauline. As they came to the Sherman Building Jenny caught sight of the new store. It was now filled with shelves and books. Why, it was going to be a library!

Jenny hurried Pauline into the elevator and down the corridor. Marge turned on her swivel chair. She was short and just a little plump. She had to stretch more than the other girls when she reached across to the second switchboard. But the most striking thing about her was her dimpled smile. Marge had the deepest dimple Jenny had ever seen.

Marge smiled at Jenny now. "Hello, honey," she said. "I'm so glad you brought Pauline with you. Trudi will be glad to have someone to play with."

"I hope she won't give you any trouble," Jenny said. "Is it all right if I leave her now? I'd like to see the new library downstairs."

"Sure, sweetie," Marge said. "Pauline and I will have a great time. And when Trudi comes, she and Pauline can play in the next room."

Until then, no doubt, Marge would hold Pauline on her lap and tell her to "plug in here, baby."

As Jenny hurried down the stairs (she did not wait for the elevator this time) she hoped that Pauline would not suddenly decide to speak into Marge's headpiece and announce, "This is Gladie, the kangaroo."

The library would not be open until Tuesday, the redheaded librarian told Jenny. But when she saw how disappointed Jenny looked, she said, "You may come in, if you like. But half the books are still in cartons."

"Could I help you unpack books and things?" Jenny asked.

The librarian smiled. "You must really love books," she said, "if you are willing to help unpack them."

"Oh, I do!" Jenny followed her into a back room.

She could start with that box, the woman said. "I am Miss Kaplan. I'll be the librarian at this branch."

Jenny introduced herself and got to work. She pulled the books out of boxes and set them on a cart. Miss Kaplan then wheeled the cart into the main room and shelved the books, while Jenny unpacked the next box onto another cart.

Jenny was unpacking a box of poetry volumes when she thought of the poem about trains.

"Miss Kaplan," she asked, "do you know a poem that tells about how the poet wants to go traveling everytime she hears a train? One part says something about imagining red cinders in the sky when she just hears the train whistle. And in the end she says she would take any train—going anywhere."

" 'Yet there isn't a train I wouldn't take . . .

no matter where it's going,'" Miss Kaplan quoted. "That poem is called 'Travel,' and it's by Edna St. Vincent Millay."

"That's how I feel sometimes," Jenny said. "Especially now."

Miss Kaplan laughed. "Thank goodness there are a few trains left to ride on. Let's see if we can find that poem." She opened another carton of poetry volumes. "I know I have it in one of my books at home. No, it's not in this box." She reached for the next carton.

"I'll tell you what we can do, Jenny," Miss Kaplan said after a bit. "I can't lay my hands on that volume. But I'm about to stop work for the day anyway. So why don't you walk home with me, and I will lend you my own book?"

Jenny considered this for a moment. Pauline would be all right with Marge. And going home with Miss Kaplan sounded like an adventure, even though a small one.

On the way home Miss Kaplan asked Jenny if she knew her niece. "Ruth Kaplan. She's in the sixth grade at Circle School." Jenny said there were two sixth grade classes. "Ruth must be in the other one."

The Kaplans lived in a brick apartment house near the school. Jenny was surprised that the apartment was so big until Miss Kaplan explained that she lived with her brother and his wife—Ruth's parents—and Mrs. Kaplan's mother.

The living room was warm and cozy. The wall on either side of the fireplace was lined with bookshelves. Miss Kaplan found the poem and Jenny read it aloud:

"The railroad track is miles away,
    And the day is loud with voices
      speaking,
Yet there isn't a train goes by all day
    But I hear its whistle shrieking.

"All night there isn't a train goes by,
    Though the night is still for sleep and
      dreaming
But I see its cinders red on the sky,
    And hear its engine steaming.

"My heart is warm with the friends I
      make,
    And better friends I'll not be knowing,
Yet there isn't a train I wouldn't take,
    No matter where it's going."

"I've always loved that one," Miss Kaplan said when Jenny had finished. "If the pull of distant places is so strong when things are fine, when her 'heart is warm with friends,' think how it must be when things are dull or unhappy."

That was exactly what she meant, Jenny said. And to herself she added, "When the heart is cold with friendship dying." Then she laughed. Andy would call her a big Gloomo, his current favorite expression.

Jenny's thoughts were interrupted by the entrance of a girl Jenny's own age. She was small, redheaded, and freckled. Her short red hair curled up slightly at the ends. Jenny wished her own straight brown hair had some curl to it.

"This is my niece, Ruthie," Miss Kaplan said. "And this is Jenny Jason."

Ruthie grinned. "Hi," she said. Jenny said hello.

"Perhaps you girls would like to visit a bit," Miss Kaplan suggested.

"Can't," Ruthie said. "I have a Hebrew class in a few minutes. It's a make-up, because I missed last weekend.

"I'm going to be a Hebrew teacher when I grow up," she said to Jenny. "And an artist. I'm going to start Art School next month. Well, I have to get going—or I'll be late. Maybe we can get together sometime soon."

"I have to go, too," Jenny said quickly. She did not want Ruth Kaplan to know that she

48

was disappointed, that she cared whether or not they had time to "visit."

Ruthie said she would ride down in the elevator with Jenny, but at the last minute discovered that she did not have her Hebrew books. "Where are they, Aunt Roz?"

"You probably left them under your bed—or someplace like that."

Ruthie laughed. "I guess I am pretty sloppy," she said. "Come on, help me look, or I'll be late for class."

Miss Kaplan sighed. "I *told* you I wouldn't chase around looking for your things any more," she said. "You will have to learn to put things in their proper places."

"Well . . . I'd better go," Jenny said. "I have to pick up my little sister. Thank you for the book, Miss Kaplan. I'll return it soon."

"You're welcome, Jenny. And thank you for helping me."

"So long," Ruthie called from behind the couch. "I'll be seeing you."

"Bye," Jenny answered. She did not have much hope of seeing Ruthie soon. Ruthie was so busy—with Hebrew school and art classes! Besides, a girl like Ruthie Kaplan, who knew exactly what she would be and do when she grew up—a Hebrew teacher *and* an artist—

would probably not have time for a new friend.

And Jenny didn't really want a *new* best friend, she told herself. What she really wanted, Jenny knew, was her old best friend, Dot. She wanted everything to be the same as it was before Dot moved and Edythe came on the scene.

Jenny went down in the elevator feeling sorry for herself.

Chapter 4

The Birthday Celebration

Thursday was Jenny's birthday. Probably nobody would even remember, she told herself. Everyone was so busy at home—Carol with her choir practice and journalism, Andy with his dog-walking business. And Dad with so many more things on his mind now that they were without a housekeeper. Even Dot probably would forget, since lately her thoughts seemed all with Edythe.

But Jenny was wrong. Both Dad and Carol remembered her birthday and were making plans.

"How would you like a birthday party at the Chinese restaurant?" Dad asked that night at dinner.

"Oh, Daddy!" Jenny exclaimed, "that's a terrific idea. How did you ever think of it?"

"As a matter of fact," Dad admitted, "I didn't. It was Carol's inspiration. She is going to stay home with Andy and Pauline, and I am going to take you and two or three of your friends to the China Door. After all, you'll be twelve—and we thought it would be a nice change from the ice cream and cake birthday parties."

"Oh, much better!" Jenny agreed. "I think it's a wonderful idea."

But on the way to school the next morning Jenny's happy mood of anticipation was suddenly clouded by the disturbing question. Whom would she invite to the birthday dinner? Dad had said two or three friends. But when you came right down to it, Jenny realized, she didn't have many friends—except Dot. One of the joys of having a best friend was that you didn't really need anyone else, even on your birthday. And when you did have a party, you and your best friend could always decide together whom to invite. Dot had always helped Jenny with her guest list, and Dot always had definite ideas on who should be included. Dot had definite ideas on everything, and Jenny was accustomed to following her friend's lead.

By the time she reached school Jenny had decided that perhaps she had been unfair when she got so angry with Dot yesterday. This celebration would be just what she and Dot needed to patch things up between them. She might also invite one of the girls from her Sunday school class. And there was one girl at school, Jean Marie Baker, whom Jenny liked.

Now that she had made up her mind, Jenny looked around eagerly to find Dot.

But Dot was not on the grounds, nor was she in the classroom. In fact, the last bell was sounding when Dot dashed through the door and slid into her seat.

Immediately after the opening exercises, Miss Blake spoke about the *Alice in Wonderland* marionette show.

"I have the sketches you turned in for the marionettes and costumes," she said, "and I will tentatively choose a principal actor and an understudy for every role. The two students chosen for each part will work together on the puppet. Both will learn lines, and both will have a chance to perform."

Miss Blake began her announcements with the smaller parts. Sometimes she named one player for a role, sometimes two.

"I am leaving some roles open," she explained. "The beginning of next month, at the start of the second term, I expect some new pupils, and I am sure they will want to be in the marionette play."

A few of the boys said they did not want parts, and they were assigned to work on the construction of the stage.

Jenny, looking over at Dot, saw that her friend was twisting her handkerchief around and around her wrist. She knew how much Dot wanted the role of Alice, and she wished hard that Dot would get it. And then Jenny had another idea. Suppose she were chosen for the understudy to Alice! Then she and Dot would be working together—and soon they would be best friends again.

Miss Blake had assigned the roles of the Duchess and the King of Hearts. Jenny, lost in her thoughts, was surprised to hear her own name called.

"Jenny Jason—for the principal of the Queen of Hearts."

"Oh, no!" Jenny protested silently.

"And the understudy for the Queen of Hearts—Jean Marie Baker."

Now all that was left were the roles of the White Rabbit and Alice. The role of Rabbit was given to a tall thin girl who giggled a great deal. And then Dot was chosen for Alice. The class let out a deep sigh and someone said, "Oh, good!" Jenny smiled and waved at her friend, but Dot was looking at the teacher and did not notice.

"Thank you, Miss Blake!" she said. "I'll work so hard!"

"I know you will, Dot," Miss Blake said.

"Who is going to be the understudy to Alice?" Jenny asked, and Miss Blake replied, "I am not deciding that now. That is one of the roles I want to leave open until the change of terms. I can always do some juggling around at that time."

This left Jenny with some hope. Perhaps she could persuade Miss Blake to take her out of the role of Queen of Hearts and let her be Dot's understudy.

The class began working on the designs for the marionettes. Jean Marie came over to Jenny's desk with her drawing of the Queen, and the two girls went to a table at the back of the room to discuss the face and costume of the puppet.

"This is going to be a great project," Jean Marie said. "Miss Blake says we're going to make papier-maché heads and cloth bodies for the puppets."

Jenny looked at her companion. Jean Marie was short and plump with one thick brown braid hanging halfway down her back. Her round eyes and small nose gave her face an almost babyish look, but Jenny knew that when Jean Marie opened her mouth to talk, this impression was quickly dispelled. Jean Marie's speech was clear and precise, and she was one of the best students in the class.

"Actually," Jean Marie was saying, "these won't be puppets, they will be marionettes. They're going to be operated with strings."

Jenny was scarcely listening. She was wondering how soon she could ask Miss Blake to change her role. Not too soon, Jenny decided—perhaps next week. Nor would she tell Dot her plan until it was all settled. The birthday dinner would be news enough for Dot today. Jenny smiled to herself. In the excitement over the marionette play, she had almost forgotten it.

Jenny's first opportunity to speak to Dot alone came after school.

"It's awfully nice of you to invite me, Jenny," Dot said when Jenny told her about the plans. "I'm glad you're not mad at me for inviting Edythe to go with us on Monday."

"Naturally, you're the first one I'm asking," Jenny concluded. "It'll be at six-thirty on Thursday."

"Thursday?" Dot sounded dismayed. "Oh, Jenny, not Thursday!"

"Of course Thursday. That's my birthday."

Dot looked down at her gym shoes. "I can't come Thursday, Jenny. That's the day we have our club meeting. We're meeting at Edythe's apartment at seven o'clock."

Jenny said nothing. She had forgotten all about the Thursday Club!

"You know," Dot added. "We meet every Thursday."

Jenny's throat felt so tight she was not sure she could answer.

"Couldn't you just this once not go to your club meeting?" she asked at last. "Just this once?"

Dot shook her head. "I really have to go. This is the first meeting, and Edythe says I'm going to get the hatbox and pin. There's even a special ceremony for new girls. . . . I'm sorry, Jenny," Dot added. "Really I am."

Jenny briefly considered changing the day of her dinner. But that would seem very odd to Dad and to Carol. Besides, Thursday was her birthday—not some other day.

"I'm sorry," Dot said again, and Jenny mumbled something and hurried off. "It's my *birthday!*" she kept saying to herself. Dot could have skipped this one club meeting.

She would tell Dad that she didn't want a

birthday dinner. She could just hear everyone asking, "Where is Dot?" What fun would it be now, anyway?

Don't be such a big Gloomo, Jenny told herself sternly as she rounded the corner near her house. She decided that the one thing she would not do was call off her birthday dinner. If inviting her other classmates would only point up Dot's absence, she could invite entirely different friends, friends who did not even know Dot. Grown-up friends, for instance. She could invite Miss Kaplan and Marge. Marge was an old friend of the family, and Miss Kaplan was a new friend of Jenny's. She turned purposefully toward the Sherman Building.

Marge said she would love to come to her party and asked Jenny if she wanted to stay and watch the operators. Normally Jenny loved to watch the operators plug cords into the switchboard and answer the calls. The most fascinating part, Jenny thought, was hearing them answer each line with a different name or number. ("Good afternoon. Bill's Garage." "Dr. Green's office; may I help you?") Jenny often wondered what would happen if an operator answered Dr. Green's office with "Morton's TV Repair."

"Thanks, Marge," Jenny answered, "but I

have to be running along. I want to invite one more guest, and then I'd better get home—so Pauline won't be alone."

"Your sister is a darling," Marge said. "She and my Trudi got along so well together yesterday. You may leave Pauline with me any time you like."

Jenny smiled. Marge was always so nice.

Jenny had to wait while Miss Kaplan charged out books for a tall woman and a little boy, and it suddenly occurred to her that she really should invite Ruthie, too. It would seem peculiar to invite the aunt and not the niece—who was her own age. Besides, Dad had said she could invite two or *three* guests.

"I would like to invite you to my birthday dinner, Miss Kaplan," Jenny said when the woman and boy departed. "And Ruthie, too. It will be at the China Door Restaurant on Thursday at six-thirty."

The librarian was delighted, and said she was sure that Ruthie would love to come, too.

Jenny returned home to find her sister Carol looking through old photographs.

"I'm looking for a picture of Grandma," she said. "So far this is all I can find."

Jenny took the snapshot from her sister. It showed a tall, thin woman and a big dog. But the woman's face was blurry, and Jenny could not tell what she looked like.

There would have to be a reshuffling of bedrooms before Grandma arrived, Carol said. Grandma would naturally want her own room. This could be arranged by giving Grandma Carol's room. "And I'll move in with you and Pauline."

"Three people will make that room awfully crowded," Jenny pointed out.

"Well, I don't like giving up my room, either," Carol said, "but it is all we can do."

"Who are you inviting to dinner on your birthday?" she asked, changing the subject completely.

Jenny told her sister all about the guests she had invited, and was grateful that Carol did not ask her, "What about Dot?"

Jenny awoke Thursday morning feeling, she told Carol, at least a whole year older.

"You *look* a year older," Carol teased, and laughed when Jenny raced to the mirror.

Of course, it was yesterday's face that looked back at her: straight dark hair, not long and not short, gray eyes and a short, straight nose. Nothing interesting here. She gathered some hair near the top of her head

into a high, short pony tail. "What do you think, Carol?"

"Oh, I like that," her sister told her. "It makes you look—well, elfin."

Elfin was not exactly how Jenny wanted to look, but at least it was different. The year-older Jenny (*day* older, rather) should be a new Jenny.

At breakfast Jenny received a birthday hug and a slim bracelet from Dad, a scarf from

Carol, and a book about dinosaurs from Andy and Pauline.

At school, Dot was waiting for her on the playground, and she handed Jenny a square box.

"Happy birthday, Jenny," she said. "I hope you have a very nice day."

"Thanks, Dot." Jenny carefully untied the ribbon and found a box of dusting powder under the pink tissue paper. "I'll love using it."

"I'm glad you like it," Dot said, and then she added, "I *am* sorry I can't be at your birthday dinner, Jenny."

"That's okay," Jenny said, and realized to her amazement that she was looking forward to her birthday dinner, even if Dot wouldn't be there.

Jenny and her father were the first to arrive at the restaurant. The proprietor directed them to a round table marked "reserved," and within a few minutes everyone was there— Marge, Miss Kaplan, and Ruthie. Jenny introduced her father to Miss Kaplan and Ruthie.

"This is delicious!" Ruthie looked up from her vegetable chop suey. "I just love lifting the silver covers and peeking inside."

Jenny, too, thought that was half the fun of eating in a Chinese restaurant.

"When I grow up," Ruthie continued, "I'm going to manage a whole string of hotels, and each dining room will be a different nationality restaurant—French, Italian, Chinese."

"I thought you were going to be an artist and a Hebrew teacher!" Jenny said.

Miss Kaplan laughed. "That was last week, Jenny. The week before she wanted to be a fashion designer—so she can go to Paris and Rome."

"What do you want to be?" The freckles stood out on Ruthie's nose as she looked at Jenny.

"I think I'd like to be a librarian," Jenny replied promptly, although she really hadn't thought of it until just this moment.

"That's good," Ruthie said.

"Why, Jenny!" Marge sounded hurt. "You told me you wanted to be a telephone operator and run an answering service. Because we are so helpful, you said."

Jenny giggled. She had said that—once.

"You could be a librarian *and* a telephone operator," Ruthie said. "There are so many wonderful things to do, you should be two things—like me."

Everyone laughed, and suddenly Jenny decided that she *did* like Ruth Kaplan.

When the waiter brought the fortune cookies, Ruthie pulled the slips of paper and pretended to read funny sayings.

"Tip the waiter," she read from her aunt's cookie slip.

"Brush your teeth three times a day," she read from another.

Jenny laughed. "Show me where it says that."

"Here, look," Ruth said. She held the paper out, but snatched it away before Jenny could read the words.

"Listen to this one." Dad held his paper and read, "Help! I'm imprisoned in a Chinese cookie factory!"

"Oh." Ruth sounded disappointed. "I was just about to pull that one."

Jenny wondered if someone might not be indeed imprisoned in a cookie factory and sending a note to get help.

"This has been a superb party," Miss Kaplan said. "I can't tell you how glad I am that you invited us."

"Wait, Miss Kaplan!" Dad said. "It isn't over yet."

A moment later there were strains of "Happy Birthday to You," and a flaming cake

seemed to be walking toward them. The cake was covered with lighted sparklers, and then Jenny could see that it was being carried by a Chinese girl about her own age. The girl greeted Ruthie warmly, and Ruthie introduced her to the others.

"This is my friend, Betty Lee," she said. "Her father owns this restaurant."

"When I saw you," Betty said to Ruth, "I asked Daddy to let me bring the cake. He hardly ever lets me help, but he said I could tonight." She giggled softly. "Ruth and I are in the same class at school," she explained to the others.

"But not for long," Ruth said.

Betty lowered her eyes and looked embarrassed. "The teacher says we laugh and joke together too much and don't concentrate on the work. She says when the new term starts, one of us will be sent to the other sixth grade class." She looked at Ruth, who dissolved into laughter.

"I'll bet she sends *me* to the other class," Ruthie said between giggles. "The teacher will want to keep Betty. She has a marvelous memory. You should hear her recite pages of poetry—by heart."

Betty Lee poked her friend. "Oh, come on!" she said.

Jenny could picture the two of them giggling together in school. She stood up.

"I'm going to cut the cake," she said to Betty. "Why don't you sit down and help us eat it?"

"I'd love to," said Betty Lee.

It was the best birthday she'd ever had, Jenny told Dad later. And then, just before Jenny went to bed, there was the cablegram. Grandma was arriving on Saturday at two fifty-five!

Chapter 5

Grandma

Jenny woke up early the next morning, full of plans for welcoming Grandma.

"Why don't we all go out to the airport tomorrow?" she asked at breakfast. "We could be a surprise reception committee."

"Of course. We must all be there to welcome Grandma," Dad said.

"Can I borrow Mr. Ellison?" Pauline interrupted. "I'm giving a French report and I need a turtle. Andy? Please!"

"Good night! What does a French report have to do with my turtle?"

"My French report is about turtles," Pauline explained patiently. "It starts, 'Voici la tortue.'"

Andy was not inclined to lend his pet turtle, named for a favorite science teacher. He

grumbled that no first-graders should be taking French and the Special Abilities classes were the baloney. But Pauline persisted, and he finally agreed, reluctantly, to let her take the turtle.

"But you must be *very* careful, Pauline. Keep him in a box."

"Oh, thank you, Andy!" Much to his annoyance Pauline hugged her brother. "Now I'll get a better grade than Gertrude."

"Who is Gertrude?" Dad inquired.

Gertrude, Pauline explained, was a new girl in class.

"I'll tell you all about how good my report is," she added to Andy, "and how mad Gertrude got—as soon as I get home from school."

But Andy, having placed Mr. Ellison in a box for Pauline, was no longer interested in her report—or in Gertrude. He had to leave immediately to see about getting a paper route, he said. "It's a good thing I got that big bike for Christmas," Andy told them. Andy's full-size bicycle was his proudest possession, and he didn't mind a bit that he had to stand to reach the pedals.

"I promised the man I'd see him before school," Andy told them. He dashed out the door, and Carol rose and slipped into her coat.

"Don't forget, Jenny," Carol said, swallowing the last of her coffee. "Bring up the laundry as soon as you come home from school." She had put the clothes into the washer before breakfast, Carol explained as she gathered her books together.

"I'll move them into the drier on my way out," she called over her shoulder, "and don't forget to bring them up. You know how angry Mrs. Cotton gets when we leave things in the laundry room."

Dad left shortly after Carol, and Jenny was on her way to school before she remembered that they had reached no decision with regard to meeting Grandma's plane.

Jenny's thoughts raced on. In addition to meeting the plane, it would be nice to have a little gift for Grandma—a sort of welcoming present. Jenny was deep in thought about the present for Grandma as she crossed into the schoolyard. She did not see Ruth at first.

"Boo!" Ruth said, linking her arm in Jenny's. "What are you—sleepwalking or something?"

"Oh, hi, Ruthie. I was just wondering about a present for my grandmother." And Jenny told Ruth about her plans to welcome Grandma.

"Now I wish I could figure out something nice to buy her," Jenny added, "that doesn't cost too much. I only have a dollar seventy-five."

Ruth had an idea. Her Grandma Fennerman crocheted edgings on linen handkerchiefs.

"She does this all the time—for herself and for gifts—and sometimes she sells them to raise money for the synagogue. She could make you any color border you want."

This sounded like a fine idea to Jenny.

"The thing is, I have to get the gift today. I

want to give it to Grandma when she gets off the plane."

"That's okay," Ruth told her. "Grandma Fennerman lives with us. She'll be home today, cooking dinner. Friday is one of the days my mother works."

So it was arranged that Jenny would meet Ruth after school and go to the Kaplan apartment.

Grandma Fennerman was taking three long loaves out of the oven when the girls arrived.

"That's a special kind of bread we have," Ruth explained. "It's called *challah,* and we always eat it on Friday night."

Jenny sniffed. The kitchen smelled of fresh bread and chicken soup, a rich, fragrant odor.

"This is my friend, Jenny," Ruth said to her grandmother. Grandma Fennerman patted Jenny's shoulder and offered the girls fresh fruit and orange juice.

As she drank her orange juice Jenny watched Ruthie's grandmother. Grandma Fennerman was small, plump and pretty. Her white hair was wound into an attractive French twist, and she moved with quick birdlike motions. When Ruthie explained about the gift for Jenny's grandmother, Grandma Fennerman went into the bedroom and returned with a deep box.

"I haven't time to make a handkerchief edging to order," she said. "There's still a lot to be done for tonight's dinner. But you may choose from the handkerchiefs in this box."

Jenny chose two. One had a beautiful turquoise border and the other was trimmed in several shades of soft pink.

As she turned to leave, Ruthie stopped her.

"I had a wonderful time at your dinner last night, Jenny. Thanks for inviting me.

"Jenny's birthday was yesterday," she explained to her grandmother, "and we had dinner at the China Door. Aunt Roz, too."

"Happy birthday, honey," Grandma Fennerman said. Then she turned to her granddaughter. "*Chinese* food! It can't be as good as my chicken and fish—and challah."

"Oh, yes, it can," Ruthie said, her eyes dancing. "It can be better. And maybe it is.

"Grandma thinks there is no cooking to compare with Jewish cooking," she added to Jenny, "especially *her* Jewish cooking."

Grandma Fennerman sniffed. "Have a fish ball," she said to Jenny, "and *you* tell me if it isn't better than any Chinese food." And she cut off a piece of fish patty and handed it to Jenny on a paper napkin.

"It certainly is *good*," Jenny said. "It's just about the best fish I ever ate." It really didn't taste like fish at all, Jenny thought. It was sweeter than most fish—and tangier. But then she had never tasted cold chopped fish before.

"Here." Grandma Fennerman handed Jenny another generous portion. "Have some more. It's good with challah." And she cut off a slice of the fresh bread.

"Not for you!" Grandma Fennerman swatted at Ruthie, who was reaching for a slice of the fish. "I don't waste my good gefilte fish on a child who teases her grandmother. Now your friend is a girl after my own heart. *She's* going to treat her grandmother properly. She's already buying a present to welcome her."

"I hope she turns out to be just like you," Jenny said. It would be wonderful, Jenny decided, to come home every day to a grandmother as soft and pretty and such a good cook as Grandma Fennerman.

Ruthie laughed and hugged her grandmother.

"I take it all back, Grandma Fennerman," she said. "Your food is the best in all the world.

It's better than Chinese cooking or French cooking—or anything."

"You're teasing again, Ruth Kaplan," Grandma Fennerman said. But she popped a bite of gefilte fish into Ruthie's mouth and laughed.

Jenny found a box for the two handkerchiefs when she got home and tied it with a pale blue ribbon. Then she found a plain white card and wrote: "To Grandmother—welcome to Jason Manor—with love, Jenny."

She was just tucking the card under the ribbon when she heard the front door slam and then her brother's voice.

"I should have known better than to trust you with anything!"

And then there was a wail from Pauline. "But it wasn't my fault!"

Jenny went into the kitchen to find Andy yelling and Pauline sobbing. Pauline had returned with an empty box hanging open at the sides, and Andy had gone back with her, tracing the streets from school. There was no sign of Mr. Ellison.

"It was Gertrude," Pauline sobbed. "That terrible Gertrude in my class. She took Mr. Ellison on the playground, and she *lost* him."

"Always blaming someone else," Andy croaked, and Jenny asked, "What's wrong with your voice, Andy?"

He had a sore throat, Andy said. But who cared about that when Mr. Ellison was missing?

"There are throat lozenges in Dad's drawer, and I'll make you some hot lemonade." Carol spoke from the doorway, where she stood with Bunny Monroe. Jenny noticed that Carol was looking exceptionally pretty. Her blond hair had blown about her face and her cheeks were pink from the cold.

"And then," Carol added, "I'll tell you some important news!"

"Tell us now," Pauline insisted, and Bunny echoed. "Tell them now, Carol. I think I'm more excited than you!"

It was just that she had been elected feature editor of her high school paper for next term, Carol explained.

"Your own sister is feature editor of the *Black and Gold!*" Bunny underscored Carol's announcement.

They all talked at once as they crowded around to congratulate Carol.

"Gertrude was the one who did it," Pauline wailed, remembering her troubles once more.

"Gertrude did *what?*" Carol asked. "And who is Gertrude?"

Jenny and Andy started to tell her the story, but were interrupted midway by a loud knock on the door. Andy opened it to a very irate Mrs. Cotton. Her fuzzy blond hair stood out from her head in little puffs and wisps, and her round face was red with anger.

"Will you young people inform me how any tenants can use the laundry room when the Jasons never remove their clothes from the drier?" She shook a finger at Carol. "You promised me, young lady, that those clothes would be out of the laundry room by three-thirty this afternoon. It is a quarter to five."

Carol turned to Jenny. "Oh, Jenny!" she said. "You didn't forget again?"

Jenny sighed. She *had* forgotten again. She had been thinking only of the gift for Grandma, and she'd gone off to Ruth Kaplan's apartment without a thought for the laundry.

"I'll—I'll take care of it right away," she said and ran for the stairs.

When Jenny came upstairs with the folded clothes, she learned that the Cottons planned to move into the apartment recently vacated by the Jeffersons.

"She said she and Mr. Cotton want to be where they can watch things more closely." Andy paused to sip his hot lemonade. "As if she doesn't snoop enough now. She only lives a few blocks away, and she's over here almost all day."

But Jenny could not be concerned about the Cottons. She was too happy thinking about Grandmother and the present that was ready for her. Even Carol's, "Jenny, you'll *have* to remember your chores" did not disturb her. Jenny hummed as she put the clothes away and whistled as she set the table for dinner. And she was delighted when Dad agreed that they should all go to meet the two fifty-five plane from New York.

Saturday morning dawned dark and sleety.

"Andy didn't go out in this terrible weather?" Dad asked at breakfast, and Carol nodded.

"I tried to talk him out of it," she said, "but it was his first day on the new paper route, and he said he *had* to go."

Dad shook his head. "He had a bad cold to start with. No doubt he'll come home really sick."

Andy did. His throat was much worse when

he came in, cold and wet. Carol insisted on taking his temperature and sent him to bed.

"There's *one* who won't be going to the airport with us," Dad said. Then he added, "Not that I'm sure any of us will be going out. With the weather the way it is, the planes may not be flying."

"But what will Grandmother *do* if her plane is grounded?" Jenny asked.

Dad smiled. "Don't you worry about your grandmother, Jenny. She'll get here some way. Train maybe, or bus. It just may take a day or so longer."

"Maybe it's clear in New York," Jenny said. She had been looking forward to greeting her grandmother *today*.

After breakfast Dad helped them move Carol's bed into Jenny's and Pauline's bedroom. Every few minutes Jenny ran to the window in the living room. The long "tower windows" gave the best view in the apartment, and if there were a spot of clear, sunny sky moving toward them, this could surely be seen first from there.

But though she looked and looked, Jenny could see nothing but gray and overcast skies.

At one o'clock Dad telephoned the airport and learned that the plane had left New York on schedule and was expected on time. All the Jasons except Andy got into Dad's car and drove toward the airport.

They arrived half an hour before the plane was due and walked up and down the passage facing the runway. At two-forty there was an announcement that the flight was forty-five minutes late due to bad weather. Jenny suddenly remembered that she had left the gift for Grandma on her dresser, but decided that she would rather give it to Grandma at home anyway.

After what seemed like hours the plane was announced. The Jasons rushed to the door and watched eagerly as the passengers walked down the portable steps that had been pushed up to the plane, and then walked briskly to the terminal. Finally they caught sight of an older woman, but she turned toward a group of people on the other side.

"Where . . . where is Grandma?" Jenny asked as the last passenger walked past them.

"It's a cinch she wasn't on that plane, Jen," her father said.

"I want to get Grandma," Pauline wailed.

No one answered. They were all disappointed, Jenny realized, including Dad. Jenny skipped around Carol and squeezed her father's arm. Dad gave her a quick hug.

The drive home seemed longer than the ride to the airport, which had been bright with anticipation. Now it might be Monday before they heard from Grandma. Perhaps she had decided to stay over in New York. Or maybe she had missed her plane in Paris.

Dad parked the car in back of the building, and the four of them traipsed wearily through the hall and up the stairs to their apartment. Even before they reached the door they heard voices and laughter.

"Andy must have company," Dad observed and put his key into the lock.

Andy did indeed have company. He was sitting propped up on the couch, leaning toward the chess table. His companion turned as they opened the door. Jenny saw a tall woman in a tweed suit. She had very short iron-gray hair that curled closely about her face, and she had a broad, delighted smile.

"Mother!" Jenny watched as her father embraced their grandmother.

But how did she get *here* when they were all waiting at the airport?

Grandma hugged them all, and everyone talked at once. Then Grandma stood back and declared that they were all much bigger than

she had imagined. Jenny thought that Grandma was taller than *she* had imagined. Grandma looked a good deal like Dad, Jenny thought. They were both tall and thin, and they both had the same broad smile.

Eventually Dad asked the question that had been puzzling Jenny. How did Grandma get to the apartment, when they were all waiting at the airport?

"Well, Howard, it was like this," Grandma began, and Dad laughed.

"Here comes one good story," he said. "Your Grandma," Dad told the children, "has an affinity for odd adventures."

"This one is quite simple," Grandma said. "I met a young man on the plane from Paris who invited me to fly with him and his mother in his own plane, from New Jersey. We landed at the lake-front airport. I took a taxi, and here I am!"

"Grandma got here about fifteen minutes after you left," Andy said proudly, "and she made me some hot milk and honey, and we've had two super chess games! I was hoping you guys would be gone even longer."

"Well, thank you, Andy Jason!" Jenny cried.

"Now, Jenny!" Dad rumpled her hair. "Let's

show Grandma the serene, pleasant side of life with the Jasons—for the first day at least."

"Yes, indeed, Jenny," Grandma said. "Birds in their little nests fall out."

Everyone laughed, and Dad said, "That's another thing about Grandma. She is never at a loss for a scrambled quotation."

After supper Grandma unpacked. However, she did not move into her bedroom until Dad agreed to move one of the other beds back in.

"Can't have three girls in one bedroom," she pronounced. "Two is a couple, more is a crowd. Three in a bedroom is never allowed."

The next question was who would room with Grandma. Jenny hoped it would be she, but Grandma settled that question by announcing that Pauline would share the bedroom with her.

"The oldest and the youngest is the way it should be," Grandma said, and that was that.

It wasn't until they were all seated in the living room that Jenny remembered the gift she had for Grandma. She ran into the bedroom to get it.

"For me?" Grandma seemed delighted. "I just love presents!"

She opened it slowly, pausing to read the card aloud. "Oh, Jenny! These are just beautiful. My favorite colors. Wherever did you find them?" Grandma gave Jenny a long hug.

Jenny was just about to tell Grandma all about Ruthie and Grandma Fennerman and the box of crochet-edged handkerchiefs, but Pauline chose that moment to announce that she was sick.

Her throat hurt, and her head ached, and she was hot and cold, Pauline declared.

"Matter of fact, I wouldn't be surprised if I got dead from this," she finished cheerfully. "Gladie is standing over there with her head in her pouch, crying. I think she's crying about me."

So they had to explain to Grandma about Gladie, and then Grandma put Pauline to bed. Pauline decided she had to have a story and no one but Grandma could tell it to her tonight, because "Gladie is listening, too."

When Pauline and Andy were finally tucked in and settled for the night, Grandma joined the others in the living room. She was thrilled, she said, to see her grandchildren—and her son—after so many years. Then she told them all about the home for orphans she had been running in France.

Dad said, "That's just like your Grandma—she starts out by lending a hand for a few days and ends up with a permanent job."

In the morning both Pauline and Andy had temperatures and were instructed to stay in bed. Jenny almost envied them the chance to stay home with Grandma.

The sun was out today and the snow and sleet completely gone. Jenny and Carol set out for the bus that would take them to Plymouth Community Church and Sunday school.

Grandma was very busy most of the day, waiting on Pauline (who said she did not want anyone else to come near her) and playing chess with Andy. Andy had decided that Grandma was the only worthy opponent in the family—she beat him about half the time. Eventually Dad said that was enough of that nonsense; Andy could read or listen to the radio. But Grandma said she enjoyed playing chess with Andy.

Carol went off with Bunny Monroe and two other girls, and Jenny sat down at the kitchen table to do her homework. It was so quiet that Jenny decided that Pauline and Andy must both be sleeping. Perhaps Grandma would

want some company now. Jenny tiptoed
toward the back of the apartment. Pauline was
asleep, and Andy was reading a book. There
was no sign of Grandma.

Dad was reading the paper in the living
room. He had not seen Grandma.

"Perhaps she went out for a little air."

Jenny wished that Grandma had asked her
to go along. She decided to put on her coat
and see if she could find Grandma downstairs.
Maybe they could go for a walk together.

Mrs. Cotton was standing at the side door,
looking out. Her lips were pulled into a
straight line, and she was scowling.

"I just saw your grandmother," Mrs. Cotton
told her. "I know it was your grandma because she was taking Andy's bicycle out of the
storage room, and I stopped her. So she told
me who she was. Then she got on Andy's bike
and rode off down the street—at quite a clip,
too."

Jenny said nothing, and Mrs. Cotton repeated, "She went off on Andy's bike—and her
an old . . . I mean, an older woman, too!"

Chapter 6

"Aw, Your Grandma
Rides Bicycles!"

Grandma came home about fifteen minutes later. She wheeled Andy's bicycle down the hall to the storage room.

Andy, in bathrobe and slippers, was waiting for her in the living room.

"Did you see Mr. Cook, Grandma?"

"Why should Grandma see Mr. Cook?" Dad asked quickly.

"Andy was worried about his paper route," Grandma began.

"That's right, Dad," Andy said. "I won't be able to deliver papers for a few days."

"Then it is up to you to find a substitute," his father told him.

"It's all taken care of, Howard," Grandma said. "I made arrangements."

Dad laughed. "I hesitate to ask what kind of arrangements."

"I arranged to deliver the papers myself until Andy is better."

Dad seemed about to speak, but Grandma hurried on. "Now don't say anything, Howard. I *want* to do it."

"But women don't deliver papers here. They don't even ride bicycles," Dad protested. "At least not very many women."

"Well, they do in France. Matter of fact, I think I'll send to France for my own."

At seven-fifteen Monday morning Grandma was out with Andy's list, delivering the papers. She returned just as Clifford Clark arrived to call for Andy.

But today Andy was not going to school. Clifford was aghast when he learned that Grandma had delivered Andy's papers for him.

"I would have done it for you, Andy," he kept saying. "Boy, a grandma who can ride a bike and deliver newspapers!"

Clifford was still talking about Andy's remarkable grandmother when he reached the schoolyard. Jenny overheard him telling the story to some boys in the playground.

Then she saw Dot and walked toward her. Perhaps this would be a good time to discuss the puppets and Jenny's desire to play understudy to Alice.

It seemed to Jenny that Dot looked uncomfortable when Jenny brought up the subject.

"But you have a *principal* role now," Dot began.

"We'd have so much fun working on a part *together*," Jenny cut in. "Remember how it was last year—when we did that duet for assembly? We rehearsed together, and we worked out the harmony part."

Dot nodded. "That was fun," she said.

"Hi, Jenny!"

Jenny looked up to see Ruth Kaplan coming toward them. Now why did Ruthie have to come along just now? Jenny wanted so much to show Dot how great it would be if the two Jays could work together once more—Jenny Jason and Dot Jefferson working together on a project. And Dot was beginning to be interested; Jenny could see that.

With a sigh Jenny introduced Ruthie to Dot. "We were just talking about our class marionette show," she said. "We're putting on *Alice in Wonderland*. And we're making our own marionettes."

"Jenny has the part of the Queen of Hearts," Dot said quickly, "and honest, it's one of the best parts."

"Oh, I don't know about that." Jenny was not pleased with the turn the conversation was taking.

"Just think what you can do with that part," Dot was saying, "even in making the puppet."

"It'd be fun to make the costume for the Queen of Hearts." Ruthie seemed to be picking up some of Dot's enthusiasm. "My Dad has some red velvet that'd be perfect, and there's some gold fringe that they use to trim draperies."

Her father, Ruth explained, was a traveling salesman for a company that manufactured fabrics for draperies and upholstery.

"And I get his discontinued samples," she said. "The patterns they stop making. To use for anything I want."

"Oh! That's great!" Dot cried. "That will make the Queen about the most interesting character in the whole puppet show."

Jenny wondered why Dot was so anxious to persuade her that the role of Queen was best. "I don't *want* to be the Queen of Hearts," she began. She was interrupted by a short boy with curly black hair, a classmate of Andy's.

"Hey, Jenny Jason!" he yelled. "Your brother has his old grandma delivering his papers!"

Two other boys echoed him. "Yeah, Jason's grandma is a paper boy!"

"Come on, guys." Clifford Clark stood near the group, looking embarrassed. "It's not that bad."

"I almost forgot that your grandmother was coming," Dot said to Jenny. "She isn't really delivering newspapers, is she?"

It hadn't sounded so . . . so odd until just

now when Dot asked the question. Before Jenny could think of an answer, the first bell rang.

Most of the morning was spent in clay sculpture, shaping the heads of the marionettes. Jenny gave the Queen's head small beady eyes and a scowling brow. She wanted to give her a large, open mouth, but Jean Marie felt that a straight, thin-line mouth would be more effective.

"I can see what you mean," Jenny said as Jean Marie reshaped the clay. She was thinking that it didn't make much difference anyway. Jean Marie could have the marionette all to herself as soon as Jenny got the role of understudy to Alice. But first she would have to persuade Dot. Jenny wondered again why Dot was resisting this. Dot was friendly enough now. She even walked part way home with Jenny at lunch time.

On the way they met Mrs. Cotton, pushing her market cart.

"If you're wondering where your grandma is," she said, and it seemed to Jenny that Mrs. Cotton actually sniffed as she said *your grandma*, "she said she was going marketing, and she rode off on that bicycle."

Jenny laughed.

"That's one way to get the marketing done," she said.

As Mrs. Cotton marched off down the street, Jenny whispered to Dot, "Maybe she's mad because Grandma didn't offer her a ride on the handlebars," and both girls laughed.

It was almost like old times, Jenny thought.

But in the days that followed Jenny did not find Grandma's bike riding very funny.

She had thought that when Grandma came, things would be different—more like having a mother around. She'd thought Grandma would always be there when they came home from school, and would straighten out their problems if they had any. But maybe Jenny was expecting too much.

Grandma loved to fix things. She fixed Carol's typewriter and Andy's electric train and even the doorknob in the lobby. Grandma always wore baggy blue coveralls when she fixed things—except when she wore faded jeans and sneakers. And Grandma liked to sing as she worked.

One thing Grandma did *not* like to do was housework. She called them all together one day and explained that household chores should be divided among members of the family—Dad excluded, of course, because he was busy earning a living.

"Grandmas find housework for idle hands," she pronounced cheerfully.

Andy would run the vacuum cleaner, Jenny was to be in charge of dusting and bringing up the laundry, Pauline would set the table, and Carol offered to do some of the laundry and part of the cooking.

Jenny was the only one who did not attack her new chores with enthusiasm. She had to be reminded twice in the next three days to bring up the laundry.

"When we all pitch in and do the chores," Andy told her, "Grandma has more time to do things for us—like fixing and repairing and stuff."

Jenny did not tell her brother that she for one would prefer that Grandma did less fixing and repairing.

When Grandma became interested in switchboards and went to work at the Answering Service, it was almost a relief. It happened this way: Marge telephoned the apartment one evening to give Dad a message. It was Grandma who answered the phone, and she spoke to Marge for quite a while before she called Dad.

"That poor girl," Grandma said to Dad

when he returned to the living room. "She can't even get out to lunch."

"What poor girl?" Dad asked.

"That Margie who runs the Answering Service. One of her day-shift operators is in the hospital and another was called home to Milwaukee. Poor Margie never went out to lunch today."

"That's a shame," Dad said.

"I told her she'll get sick herself if she isn't careful. But it isn't so easy to find someone to work a switchboard."

Dad said nothing, and Grandma continued. "I've worked a small switchboard. We had one at the orphanage."

Dad laughed. "When are you starting to work at the Answering Service, Mother?" he asked. "Tomorrow morning?"

"How did you know I was starting to work there?" Grandma asked.

"I can tell when one of your 'helping out' projects is coming on," Dad said.

"I always say," Grandma said cheerfully, "a helping hand leads to all roads."

So the very next morning Grandma went to work at the Answering Service. All that week she dressed in her brown tweed suit each morning and left the apartment when Jenny and Pauline and Andy went to school. Grandma worked from nine until twelve and from one until four-thirty. She was home by the time the children came home for lunch, and she was back at the apartment half an hour after they got home from school.

On Sunday Jenny spent most of the day with Ruth Kaplan and Betty Lee. The three girls went ice skating and then saw a travel movie at the Art Museum. After the movie there was a short puppet show, and that reminded Ruthie that she had some red velvet for the Queen's costume. The two girls said good-bye to Betty at the bus stop, and Jenny went home with Ruth.

Grandma Fennerman was in the living room sewing, and she was delighted to see Jenny. Jenny thought once again how pretty and soft looking Ruthie's grandmother was.

"Why don't we see you here more often?" Grandma Fennerman asked Jenny. Then she said to Mrs. Kaplan, "Jenny is a girl who appreciates good cooking." Grandma Fennerman patted Jenny's arm. "You'll have to come to dinner. How about next Friday?"

Mr. and Mrs. Kaplan seconded the invitation, and Jenny said she would ask her grandmother. Mrs. Kaplan looked like a younger version of Grandma Fennerman, with the same delicate features and trim hairdress. But Mrs. Kaplan's hair was a clear black, while her mother's was all white. Ruthie's father was a big man, with sandy hair and a quick smile.

When Jenny arrived home, Andy and Pauline were having a loud, bitter argument about Andy's turtle, Mr. Ellison, and Jenny forgot all about her invitation to the Kaplans.

It was Monday before Jenny thought of it again. She came home from school to find Grandma taking apart the sewing machine.

"Are you all finished at the Answering Service?" Jenny asked.

"Gracious, no," Grandma told her. "But one of the operators is back and things are not so desperate. So now I have better hours. I don't start until nine-thirty, and I'm finished at three."

She would, Grandma said, be working at the Service for at least another month—until Helen, the second operator, was back at work.

"That's very nice of you, Grandma," Jenny said.

"Not at all," Grandma told her. "I just love working the switchboard. It's fun to say, 'Good morning, Gert's Beauty Shop,' or 'Good afternoon, Frederick's School of Dance.' It makes me feel as if I *were* Gert or Frederick. For the moment, anyway."

Jenny laughed. "I always thought that would be great fun," she said. Then she remembered that she wanted to ask Grandma whether she could have dinner with the Kaplans on Friday night. Grandma readily agreed.

"A friend to visit is a friend indeed," she said. "Would you like to see what the motor of a sewing machine looks like?"

Before Jenny could reply, there was the sound of screaming at the front door, and then Pauline dashed in and flung herself at Grandma.

"Andy says Mr. Ellison is dead because I lost him. He says I killed Mr. Ellison."

"Nonsense," Grandma said. "Turtles don't die so easily. They pull their heads inside their shells and sit for centuries, just thinking."

Grandma, Jenny realized, had heard the sad story of Mr. Ellison many times. Andy missed his pet, and every once in a while he reminded Pauline of her carelessness.

"Don't you worry about Mr. Ellison, lambie," Grandma was saying. "*I* will search for him, and grandmas know how to find turtles."

Pauline stopped crying instantly and smiled

98

at Grandma, and Jenny went off to work on her puppet costume.

The costume was beginning to take shape, and everyone in Miss Blake's class admired the red velvet.

"Do you think Ruthie has a nice blue for Alice?" Dot asked one day. "I just have this old piece and it's too faded."

"Gee, I don't know, Dot," Jenny said. "But I can ask her. I'm going there Friday for dinner."

Ruthie could not find a plain blue in her box of "discontinueds," as she called them. They would ask her father after dinner.

Jenny watched as Mrs. Kaplan lit the Sabbath candles in the tall brass candlesticks. The candlesticks had belonged to *her* grandmother, Grandma Fennerman explained.

"This is the *Kiddush*," Ruthie whispered to Jenny as her father held up his wine cup and began to chant.

Grandma Fennerman was very proud of her dinner—and rightly so. But Jenny wished she did not watch so closely and urge second helpings so persistently.

Ruthie was evidently used to her grandmother's urging. "If I burst from overeating,

Grandma, who will be around to praise your cooking?"

After dinner Ruthie's Aunt Roz said, "I've missed you at the library, Jenny."

Jenny explained that she had been busy with her marionette costume. This reminded the girls of the blue fabric. Mr. Kaplan did not have any solid blue, but he said there might be some at his office.

"I'll see that you have a fine piece of Alice-in-Wonderland blue by Monday night," he said.

Mr. Kaplan was as good as his word. Ruthie called for Jenny before school Tuesday morning and handed her half a yard of sky-blue polished cotton, but then the girls got into a discussion with Andy about Mr. Ellison, and they left the fabric on the dining room table.

"I'll bring it tomorrow for sure," Jenny told Dot before class. "You'll love it. It's just the perfect blue for Alice. And I'll help you make the costume," Jenny added.

"That's okay, Jen," Dot said quickly. "I'll make it."

Jenny said nothing. She planned to speak to Miss Blake today about changing parts. Perhaps after she had her approval, Dot would warm up to the idea of working with Jenny on the role of Alice.

Miss Blake seemed surprised when Jenny put the request to her.

"Why, Jenny," she said, "I thought you were pleased with your role. Let me think about this a little while."

Jenny reached home in low spirits. She could not understand Dot's lack of enthusiasm for her desire to play understudy to Alice. And she could not understand why Miss Blake hesitated. After all, what difference could it make to Miss Blake what role Jenny had?

Grandma was in front of the house when Jenny reached home. She was wearing her blue coveralls, a man's leather jacket, and a fur cap. She was fixing the tire of a bicycle while half the children in the neighborhood looked on.

"Hi, Jenny," she called. "Go right upstairs; I'll be there soon."

Jenny couldn't go up fast enough. It embarrassed her to see her grandmother in that costume. She poured herself a glass of milk and took three cookies from a package. She was just finishing the second one when the doorbell rang. It was Dot Jefferson.

"Oh, hi, Dot. I'm so glad you came!" she

called gaily. But then the joy and good feeling fell away. Behind Dot was Edythe Fisher!

"Come . . . come on in," Jenny said without enthusiasm. She led the way into the living room.

"Say, Jenny," Edythe began, "who on earth is that crummy looking woman in front of your apartment? She looks weird, and she's fixing some bicycle and singing at the top of her voice."

Jenny groaned to herself. Why did Grandma have to be outside in front of the apartment just when Dot and Edythe came by? Why couldn't she still be at the Answering Service? She always looked presentable when she went to work. Or better yet, why couldn't she be in the kitchen baking, like Grandma Fennerman—or any other self-respecting grandma? That's what grandmas were supposed to do—not run around in coveralls fixing flat tires for neighbors' bikes!

Aloud she said, "That's my grandmother!" and her voice sounded defiant and loud even to her own ears.

"You're kidding!" Edythe said. "That's—your—grandmother?"

As if to dispel any doubts on the subject, the door opened and Grandma herself appeared in the doorway.

"Grandma, I want you to meet some friends of mine."

Grandma pushed some wisps of hair under her fur cap. She was grinning.

"I want you to meet Dot Jefferson and Edythe Fisher," Jenny said. "This is my grandmother, girls."

The two girls mumbled, "How do you do," and Grandma said, "Hello, girls," and "Have to find my 3-in-1 oil," and disappeared into the back of the apartment.

"We can't stay," Edythe said. "We came to get the blue material for our Alice costume."

"Just a minute," Jenny said. She went into the dining room and found the fabric. She wondered why Dot didn't wait until tomorrow—when Jenny would have brought the material to school. And she wondered why Edythe had to come along and act so important about everything. She had even said, "*our* Alice costume."

Jenny did not have to wait long to find out. When she offered the package to Dot, it was Edythe who reached for it.

"Thank you," she said. "Dot and I decided that it would be a good idea if we both worked on the costume afternoons and evenings this week. Then next week we can show it to Miss Blake."

103

Jenny looked blank, and Edythe added, "Oh, didn't you know? I'm transferring to your school the beginning of the new term, and the principal told my mother that I could be in Miss Blake's class—with Dot."

Chapter 7

Understudy to Alice

Jenny glanced at Dot again, but Dot seemed to have found a spot on the carpet that was fascinating her. She must have known about this a long time. All the time she had been telling Jenny how fine the role of Queen was, Dot was planning to help Edythe get the role that Jenny really wanted.

Edythe, ignoring the strained silence of the other two, chattered on about Miss Milton and why her school was no longer superior.

It was at this moment that Grandma looked into the living room.

"If Pauline or Andy should be asking for me, tell them I'm off on a search for Mr. Ellison. And this time I'm going to find him."

Naturally Edythe wanted to know who Mr. Ellison was.

"Just . . . just someone," Jenny began. The very last thing in the world she wanted was to get into a discussion of the turtle with Edythe Fisher.

But Grandma had no such reservations. She told them all about Mr. Ellison, and the three went out the front door together. Jenny, looking out of the front tower window, could see Grandma getting on Andy's bicycle and waving good-bye to the two girls.

Grandma was right about one thing. She did not return empty-handed. Pauline was delighted to see a turtle in Andy's terrarium, but Andy himself was skeptical.

"That turtle is not Mr. Ellison. Mr. Ellison was bigger than that, and he had more green in his shell."

The turtle was actually Mr. Ellison's brother, Grandma told them. So he was *a* Mr. Ellison, although not *the* Mr. Ellison.

"Grandma probably figures all turtles are brothers," Jenny observed to Carol later. "But she goes to a lot of trouble to keep Pauline happy."

Carol said Pauline had been brooding about the turtle. "Now she says *the* original Mr. Ellison is at his brother's house, while the brother is here."

In the days that followed Pauline did seem happier. But she still had problems with Gertrude, who sat in front of her in class. Gertrude pushed her, pinched her, and untied her sashes.

"And she shakes the blackboard erasers in my face," Pauline recited.

"Why don't you ask the teacher to change your seat?" Carol suggested.

"I don't want to. I love Gertrude, even if she is bad." And then she added wistfully, "I just wish she'd be good sometimes.

"You know what?" Pauline continued. "I'm going to take Doggy to see Gertrude. Doggy will scare her, and she'll be good sometimes."

Jenny laughed. Doggy was the small pugnacious bulldog recently acquired by the Cottons. The dog yipped constantly, but he never bit.

The first day of the new semester was cold and clear. Only a few other students were in her classroom when Jenny arrived before the first bell. She noticed with surprise that Ruthie Kaplan was seated in the front row, regarding Jenny with dancing eyes.

"Ruthie! What are you doing here?"

"Waiting for you to ask me," Ruthie

laughed. "I was transferred to this class. Miss Elliott said she was going to separate Betty Lee and me—and she did.

"I've known about it since yesterday, but I wanted to surprise you," Ruthie added.

She certainly was surprised, Jenny admitted. But even as she told Ruthie how great it was that she was transferred into Miss Blake's sixth grade, Jenny watched the door with a sinking feeling. Any minute now Edythe Fisher would walk into the room arm in arm with Dot.

And as Jenny expected, Edythe made a grand entrance. Dot introduced her to Miss Blake, and Edythe announced in a voice loud enough for everyone to hear, "I'm the friend Dot told you about, Miss Blake. I'm the one she wants to play the role of Alice with her."

Jenny could feel the questioning eyes of Ruthie and Jean Marie, and she wished she had not been so frank about wanting the role herself.

"It is not up to Dot to select her understudy," the teacher was saying. "One of the girls in this class has expressed an interest in the part." She concluded by asking Dot, Edythe, and Jenny to see her during recess.

At recess Miss Blake informed the three girls that she felt the matter should be settled among themselves. Jenny, who by this time was terribly sick of the whole business, said that Edythe could have the part; she would stick to the role of Queen. It wasn't worth fighting about.

"I'm glad," Miss Blake replied. "I think in the long run you'll be more satisfied with the role you have."

Miss Blake left the room then, and Jenny started back to her seat. But Dot called to her.

"I'm sorry you're angry, Jen. But I did try to tell you not to plan on the Alice part. You have a perfectly good part, and there was no reason for you to want the Alice one. No reason."

Only that you and I could work together and maybe get to be best friends again, Jenny told herself silently.

Jean Marie and Ruth both seemed to sense that Jenny was depressed.

Jean Marie asked her about it when they were working on their puppet.

"You seem so—well, so upset since recess. What happened?"

Much to her own surprise Jenny found herself telling the story to Jean Marie.

"It's not that I don't want to work with you, Jean Marie," Jenny ended quickly. "But you know how Dot and I have always worked together on projects."

"I guess Dot is the kind of person who can only be good friends with one person at a time," Jean Marie said slowly.

Jenny just stared at Jean Marie, and the girl continued. "Well, there are people like that. They have to spend all their time with one friend."

Jenny thought about this. She couldn't see what was wrong with having one best friend. She had always wanted to spend all her time with Dot, and had believed that Dot felt the same way about her.

"And then," Jean Marie was saying, "then sometimes they change, and they find another friend. And it's too bad for the first one. Besides," Jean Marie concluded, "maybe it's for the best. The Queen of Hearts is a much better part."

And at noon Ruthie invited Jenny to go to the library with her. "Aunt Roz is having that special book program on Wednesday. It might cheer you up."

Ruthie asked no questions, and Jenny

offered no explanation. "Thanks," she told Ruthie. "I'd like to go with you."

At lunch Grandma asked Jenny if she would watch Pauline after school for the next few days. "I'm working later again," Grandma said.

Jenny said she would. Then she asked whether someone else was sick at the Answering Service.

"Oh, no," Grandma said. "Everything is fine now. I leave at noon all this week."

"I'll bet you've taken on another job, Grandma," Andy said. "I'll bet you're on another 'helping out' project."

"You might say I'm on loan," Grandma began. She was interrupted by the telephone bell.

The call was for Jenny. Miss Kaplan was calling to ask Jenny if she would read the poem "Travel" at the library program. Jenny said she would.

On Wednesday Jenny walked to the library with Ruth and Betty. They took Pauline with them.

Betty said she had to stop at the restaurant first. "My mother hurt her arm day before yesterday, and she's had to stay home and put heat treatments on it. So I might have to stay and help."

"You mean you couldn't go to the library program—even for an hour?" Ruth asked. She seemed quite disappointed.

"Let's stop and see," was all Betty would say.

The girls waited in the China Door restaurant while Betty went into the kitchen. She came out in a few minutes, giggling.

"Guess who is chopping vegetables in our kitchen?"

Before they could answer, the door to the kitchen swung open again and a tall figure in a white cap and huge white apron came into the dining room. It took Jenny a minute to recognize her grandmother.

Grandma was grinning broadly. "How do you like my new uniform, Jenny?" she asked.

"Is . . . is *this* your new job?" Jenny gasped.

"I started to tell you at lunch," Grandma said. "I'm on loan here for a few hours in the afternoon—just this week, until Mrs. Lee can come back."

"And I *can* go to the library for an hour," Betty told them. "Thanks to your Grandma!"

The program at the library was well attended. Many of the boys and girls from school were there, including Edythe and Dot. Jenny read the poem "Travel," and a librarian from downtown talked about "Travel Through Books" and showed a travel movie.

Afterward Pauline and Jenny selected books to take out, and Ruth found a book on art. Jenny was standing in line between Pauline and Ruth when she realized that Edythe and Dot were in the line behind her. Ruth Kaplan chose that moment to tell about Grandma Jason.

"There was Jenny's grandmother," Ruth said, "in that enormous white apron and cap. She had been chopping vegetables in the restaurant kitchen since one o'clock, and Betty could come to the library program after all."

Edythe looked over at Jenny.

"I know your grandmother fixes bikes, and I've even seen her riding around on one. But I didn't know she works in a restaurant. How funny!"

"She doesn't really," Jenny began.

"She does today," Ruth said. "And tomorrow and the next day. I think it's wonderful, Jenny, the things your grandma does!"

But now Jenny did not think it was wonderful at all.

"I wish Grandma wouldn't do these things," Jenny complained to Carol that evening. "Like working in the restaurant and delivering newspapers and fixing bikes. It's no fun when Edythe says, 'How funny!'"

Edythe would naturally go out of her way to be mean, Carol said. "And Grandma's behavior is not so peculiar as you might think. Why, in France everyone rides around on bicycles, even grandmothers."

"Do they also fix roller skates and work in restaurants?" Jenny asked.

Carol had to admit they probably did not. But she added that while Grandma wasn't quite the way they had expected, they'd better get used to her the way she was.

The conversation ended when Pauline walked into the kitchen and announced that she was going to call up Gertrude.

Jenny giggled. "It sounds as if she's going to call up the Marines," she said to Carol.

Carol laughed. "Maybe she's going to call up Gertrude for active mischief duty."

Pauline, ignoring her sisters' comments, was dialing.

"There's no answer," Pauline said presently.

"I would think," Jenny mused, "that you

would have enough of Gertrude without calling her up."

"She's my friend," Pauline said. "I like her—even if she is bad."

"Black-hearted Gertrude," Carol muttered and turned back to her work. She had to meet Bunny at the library in a few minutes, she told Jenny. Jenny watched her sister gather her books together, thinking how lucky Carol was to have a friend like Bunny to do things with. Why, Bunny was almost like Carol's sister, the way she was at the apartment every time Jenny turned around.

Work on the marionettes and the play absorbed so much of Jenny's thoughts and energy in the days that followed that she had little time to worry about Grandma's embarrassing behavior.

Ruthie tried out for and got the role of Mock Turtle and made an expressive face for her puppet.

By the next week almost all of the puppets were completed, and the rehearsals started in earnest. Jenny began to enjoy her role as Queen. Whenever she shouted, "Off with his head!" pulling the strings of her marionette to make the Queen's arms wave, everyone laughed. One of the funniest scenes of all was

Ruthie's Mock Turtle, singing "in a voice choked with emotion" the song "Soup of the Evening."

By the second week in March Miss Blake announced that they were almost ready to present *Alice in Wonderland* from the puppet stage of Circle School.

"I have told Miss Cartwright that we would like to give our performance on Friday afternoon, April first," she said.

The principal approved the date and asked that the performance be repeated for the younger children on the following Monday.

"This will give our understudies a chance to perform, too," Miss Blake told the class. "Remember—principals on Friday, April first. Understudies will perform the following Monday. Be sure to invite your parents for the day *you* will perform."

As Jenny was leaving the school building, Edythe stopped her.

"You aren't going to invite that gooney grandmother of yours to the class puppet play, are you?" Edythe asked. "She might do something real crazy—like climb up on the stage and fix the lights or something." She nudged Dot, who laughed nervously.

"Or," Edythe added, "she might come in that awful blue suit she wears."

Jenny tossed her head. "Of course I'm going to invite my grandmother," she said. "And don't you worry about the blue coveralls. Why, she has an old sweatshirt with a hood that looks even sharper. Maybe she'll wear that."

For once Edythe Fisher had nothing to say. Jenny watched as Edythe and Dot walked out of the school and down the walk.

Not for the world would Jenny admit that she was even more concerned than Edythe about what Grandma might do or say.

Chapter 8

Plans for Grandma

There must be some way, Jenny told herself over and over, to get Grandma to act like— well, like other grandmothers. Now that she was no longer needed at the Answering Service or the China Door Restaurant, Grandma was back at work fixing bicycles and roller skates.

Although Jenny pondered the problem for many days, it was something Ruthie said that gave her the idea. Grandma Fennerman was baking for her synagogue Sisterhood. The Sisterhood was sponsoring a Purim carnival later in the month and Ruthie's grandmother was baking all kinds of delicacies and storing them in the Kaplan freezer.

"Grandma works all day for that Sisterhood," Ruthie said.

But that was it, Jenny told herself. If she could get *her* grandma interested in some worth-while church or community activities, perhaps she would forget about fixing things and riding bicycles.

Although Grandma occasionally went to church with Jenny and Carol on Sunday mornings, she had never been to the Ladies' Circle meetings. Jenny, deciding to take matters into her own hands, stopped in to see Dr. Anderson on the very next Sunday—before Sunday school.

Jenny explained that her grandmother had come from France to make her home with them. She did not know many people in town, Jenny said.

"And I thought . . . well, it might be nice if Grandma got to know some of the women in the Ladies' Circle."

The minister was very kind. He would personally see that Grandma was invited to the next Ladies' Circle meeting.

"We have many older ladies who are active in our church work," he said. "As active as their health permits."

Jenny could tell that Dr. Anderson had a picture of Grandma as an old lady, shy and delicate, but she did not see how she could correct this impression without telling too much. So she thanked the minister for his help and hurried off to class.

On Tuesday Grandma received a telephone call from the minister's wife, and on Friday Andy reported that Grandma was "at some church meeting."

During the next ten days Grandma spent a good deal of time at the church. Many days Jenny came home from school to find a note on the kitchen table saying, "I am at the church —Grandma" or "Will be at the Andersons' most of the afternoon."

Meanwhile Mrs. Cotton had reluctantly agreed to redecorate the Towers Apartments. Jenny returned home one day to find a painter working in the front hall.

"We'll be getting to your apartment one of these days," the landlady said, and Jenny raced upstairs.

Carol was home from school, but the door to their bedroom was closed and Jenny heard angry voices coming through the door—her sister's and Bunny's.

"But don't you see, Bunny," Carol was saying, "I'm new on the staff, and I really don't have anything to say about who is invited."

Bunny's answer was muffled, and as she

turned away from the door Jenny heard Carol say, "I'm sorry you feel that way, Bunny."

It was dinnertime before Jenny could tell her sister about the painting, and then right after dinner Dr. Anderson dropped by to see Grandma. The minister spent most of his time telling them all how valuable Grandma was to the Plymouth Church Tidings Committee. In fact, he said with a smile, Grandma *was* the committee.

The Church Tidings was a bi-weekly mimeographed newsletter, and until ten days ago it had been put out—in a haphazard fashion—by the overworked office secretary. But the current issue had been written and mimeographed —singlehanded—by Grandma.

"She even delivered some of the issues herself," Dr. Anderson told them, and Jenny could well believe it.

It seemed that Grandma had seen the secretary struggling with the Tidings the day she went into the church for a Ladies' Circle meeting.

"I never did get to that meeting," Grandma said, laughing. "I was so interested in the Tidings that I stayed right in the office, working on it."

Jenny sighed. "Didn't you get to any of the meetings, Grandma?" she asked.

Dr. Anderson chuckled. "There was one meeting—it was really a tea Mrs. Anderson gave at the parsonage. But your grandmother came early and one of my youngsters had broken a toy. Your grandmother went out to the kitchen with him to fix it. It was a wagon, I believe. And after that she just stayed in the kitchen, fixing things. She fixed our toaster— and the oven door that hasn't closed properly in years."

"You can bake your cake and eat it, too, if the early bird fixes the stove," Grandma said. "I had fun doing it."

"So we gathered," Dr. Anderson said.

Jenny was disappointed. She could see that the minister was very pleased with himself— and with Grandma. But as far as Jenny was concerned the whole thing was a failure. She had pinned her hopes on the Ladies' Circle influencing Grandma to become more like other grandmothers.

As the day of the marionette play approached, Jenny found herself becoming more and more apprehensive. I just hope, Jenny told herself, that Grandma doesn't decide to sing while she's in school. Jenny could just imagine the looks on her classmates' faces.

As it turned out, Jenny's worries were for

nothing. The puppet play was performed without incident, and Grandma was indistinguishable from the other mothers, aunts, and grandmothers who attended.

The production was repeated by the understudies for the younger children on Monday. Watching Jean Marie play the part of the Queen, Jenny was glad that she had stayed with that part. It *was* a more stimulating role than that of Alice. And then Jenny had another flash of understanding: working with Jean Marie was more challenging and interesting than working with Dot Jefferson. As understudy for Dot, Jenny would have fallen into the old familiar pattern, with Dot taking the lead and Jenny following along with whatever her best friend suggested.

Jenny thought that it was a very fine and exciting performance. She was especially delighted with the way Jean Marie played the Queen. They had worked out their interpretation of the part together, and it gave Jenny a feeling of pride and accomplishment to watch Jean Marie's performance.

"I wonder if we were that good last week," the girl next to Jenny asked. "The understudies are doing a great job."

Dot answered from the row behind them,

and it seemed to Jenny that Dot sniffed. "We were much better," she said.

Ruthie, who played Mock Turtle both times (there was no understudy for this part), claimed that both performances were great.

The school authorities must have agreed with her because on Wednesday Miss Blake announced that the class had been invited to perform at three different elementary schools in the next few weeks. "And I understand there are even more invitations coming," she added.

There were. The most exciting invitation came from the Cleveland Museum of Art. Miss Blake's class, the letter read, was invited to put on its *Alice in Wonderland* play on Saturday morning, April thirtieth.

"I'm sure we all realize," Miss Blake told them, "that this is a real honor."

There was just one problem. The girl who had the role of the Duchess would be out of town that weekend, and there was no understudy for this role. It was a long part for someone new to memorize. Besides that, each of the boys and girls in the class had his own role to handle.

"I have a friend in the other sixth grade class who has a marvelous memory," Ruth said, and Jenny knew she was talking about Betty Lee. "She memorizes long poems in a flash, and I'll bet she would learn the part of the Duchess for us."

Miss Blake said it would be a lifesaver if she would, and Ruth was sent across the hall to ask Betty Lee. Ruthie came back in a few minutes. Betty had readily agreed to learn the part.

It was Jean Marie who first got the idea for a cast party. She talked it over with Ruth and Jenny, and the three of them stayed in at recess to discuss their plans with the teacher.

The *Alice in Wonderland* marionette play was so much fun—and so successful—Jean Marie said, that it was only fitting that there be some kind of celebration. "A party for the cast," she concluded.

Miss Blake thought this was a fine idea. "After the performance at the Art Museum," she suggested. "Perhaps the next Monday."

Ruthie thought the party should not be at school. "If we have it at school, it will turn into just another school affair, like a Valentine's Day party or a Washington's Birthday celebration—with a few games and some cookies."

Even Miss Blake agreed.

"But if we have it in one of our homes . . ." Jean Marie seemed to be thinking aloud, ". . . it will be *ours* and we can give it a real party atmosphere. I was thinking," Jean Marie added, "that we could ask the kids to contribute whatever they'd like, and the three of us could . . . well, co-ordinate things."

"We could have the party at my house," Jenny offered.

The minute the words were out of her mouth, she was sorry. Grandma! How would she act at a party?

"Of course, I'll have to ask my folks," Jenny added.

But Jean Marie and Ruth seemed not to hear. They were delighted with the whole idea and thought Jenny's apartment would be a perfect place. And Miss Blake seemed to be heartily in favor of the whole plan.

Right after recess the teacher discussed the proposed party with the class. The boys and girls liked the idea immediately. Committees were appointed for games and refreshments. Ruth said she was sure her grandmother would bake cakes and cookies. Jean Marie and a girl named Karen were also appointed to the Food Committee.

Everyone loved the idea of a party. Only Edythe had an objection.

"I'm not sure we should have the party at Jenny's," she began, but Ruthie cut her short.

"I can't think of a better place," she declared loyally, and Jenny winced.

"I'll . . . I'll have to ask my grandmother's permission first," she said, but Ruthie waved the objection aside.

"Oh, you know your grandma will say yes."

And Grandma did, of course.

"I knew she would," Ruthie said the next day. "Your grandma is wonderful."

And Jenny, who did not know whether she was glad or sorry that Grandma had given permission, said nothing.

And then everything began to go wrong. It all started on Friday morning. The painter was scheduled to start work on their apartment on Monday, and Carol decided that this would be the weekend to clean out drawers and closets.

"We'll have to empty out the closets for the painter," she said, "and this way there will be less to put back."

Carol, popping in and out of the apartment on her many trips to the laundry room, paused long enough to give instructions to various members of the family. Andy was to get his insect and moth collection into boxes. Pauline must clean her toy shelves. And this would be a good time to clean the terrarium and give Mr. Ellison, the turtle, a fresh, neat home.

Carol's parting words were to Jenny. "Be sure to bring up the laundry—right after school." She gathered up her books and dashed out.

And then, before Jenny could get her own coat on, Carol was back. It was raining, and she needed a rainhood to protect her freshly set hair.

Perhaps Jenny would have remembered the laundry if it had not been for Dot Jefferson. The rain stopped about the middle of the afternoon, and Jenny was halfway home from school when she heard her name called. She turned to see Dot running to catch up to her.

"Jenny!" Dot called. "Jenny, wait for me!"

Dot, it turned out, was on her way to the library and did not want to go alone.

"I thought maybe you'd go with me, Jen. You know the librarian."

"Sure," Jenny said. "I'd be glad to."

While Dot was looking over two different editions of *Alice in Wonderland*, Miss Kaplan showed Jenny a biography of Edna St. Vincent Millay, and a new group of her poems. Jenny could take the books, the librarian said, even though she did not have her library card.

"Why did you want to see two more editions of *Alice?*" Jenny asked Dot as the two girls left the library. "I should think you'd have enough of that story in school."

"I wanted to see the illustrations," Dot said. "To settle an argument I had with Edythe about how Alice should look in the last scene. Edythe says she should be standing up tall, and I say she should be crouched down."

"Did you find an illustration?" Jenny asked.

"Yes," Dot told her. "And I was right. But I don't know if it'll do any good. Edythe can be so . . . so mulish."

Jenny wondered about this, but Dot had nothing more to say until they were almost in front of the Towers Apartments, and then she suddenly grabbed Jenny's arm.

"Jenny . . . Jenny, I have to tell you something."

"Sure," Jenny said, but Dot, looking up and down the street, seemed reluctant to begin.

"Something in confidence—just between us," she said. "Not here."

"We could talk in my room," Jenny told her. All the way upstairs Jenny wondered what on earth Dot could be planning to confide.

The girls opened the door to the Jason apartment to find Carol, Andy, and Grandma gathered around Mrs. Cotton. The landlady was holding a pile of something white.

Why, it was their laundry. Jenny felt a wave

of panic as she remembered. *She* was to have brought up the laundry—right after school.

"I'm real sorry," Mrs. Cotton was saying, and Jenny thought that she did not sound a bit sorry. "But you people will have to wash most of this stuff over." She put the bundle down on the dining room table, and Jenny could see that the towels and shirts had black, muddy marks on them.

"I had to take these out of the drier—finally," Mrs. Cotton said, "so that the other tenants could use it. And then Doggy jumped up on the table. . ."

And it had been raining, Jenny finished silently, and Doggy's paws did the rest. Of course Doggy should never have been allowed in the laundry room, but it would be useless to tell that to Mrs. Cotton. Jenny could almost guess what the landlady's next words would be.

She was right. "If you people would take up your laundry when you should . . . I left it in the drier until almost four o'clock."

"Oh, Jenny!" Carol sounded exasperated. "Jenny, this was *your* job. We were counting on you. I had a class meeting, and Grandma was at the church office all day."

"No use crying over dirty laundry," Grandma misquoted cheerfully. "Just take these things back down and wash them again, Jenny."

"I . . . I will in a little while," Jenny said. "Dot and I have to . . . to talk about something."

"*Right now!*" Carol's tone was sharp and Jenny looked up in surprise. "You should learn responsibility."

"Carol is right," Grandma seconded. "Responsibility is the mother of accomplishment."

Jenny sighed. She turned to tell Dot that perhaps they could talk together in the laundry room while Jenny was rewashing the clothes, but Dot was gone. Slowly Jenny collected the laundry and took it downstairs.

Now she might never learn what Dot wanted to tell her. Maybe Dot wanted to be her best friend again, and now the chance might be gone forever. Remembering how everyone had jumped on her made Jenny so angry that she closed the door of the washer with a bang.

While she waited for the washing cycle to finish, Jenny blamed everything on Grandma.

The whole problem, she decided, was that her grandmother was so busy helping other people—like the secretary at the church or

Marge at the Answering Service or the Lees at the restaurant—that she had no time for her own grandchildren. If Grandma had been home *she* could have taken the laundry upstairs, and then none of this would have happened. If only Grandma were like Grandma Fennerman, Jenny wouldn't have to worry about things like bringing up the laundry. Besides, there would be homemade cake and cookies in the house to offer her friends.

By the time all clothes and towels were washed, dried, and folded, Jenny had made up her mind. She was going to ask Mrs. Fennerman to take Grandma Jason in hand and show her the things a grandma *should* do.

After dinner Jenny went to the telephone, but somehow she could not bring herself to make the call. Once she did dial the number, but when Ruthie answered, Jenny pretended she had called only to talk about the marionette play.

She could not *tell* Grandma Fennerman her problem, but maybe she could write her a letter. There was no one in the kitchen and before she could change her mind Jenny gathered pen and paper and sat down at the table.

"Dear Mrs. Fennerman," she began. "I hope I can explain this to you . . ." She concluded by saying, "So if you will get to know my grandma, maybe you can show her how different she is, and get her to be more like you, because that's how I would like her to be." Then she added, "P.S. Please don't tell anyone about this letter."

Afterward Jenny was to tell herself that the reason she not remember to put a stamp on the envelope and mail the letter was that she really knew all along—somewhere in a corner of her mind—that the whole thing was wrong. But now, seeing Carol come into the kitchen, Jenny slipped the envelope into her library book.

"Jenny, aren't you ever going to clean out your closet?" Carol asked. "The painter will be starting here next week, and I should think you'd be anxious to get ready for him. *You're* the one who is going to have a party. I just don't know what's gotten into you lately."

"And I don't know what's gotten into *you!*" Jenny flared. "When you all jumped on me this afternoon, Dot just went away—and it's the first time she's been in our apartment in months."

"If a little family argument scared her off, it's no great loss," Carol said.

"That's easy for you to say, Carol Jason! You have a best friend. You have Bunny Monroe!"

Jenny was unprepared for her sister's outburst.

"Don't talk about Bunny Monroe to me! I'm getting so sick of her I don't know what to do. That girl won't let me breathe!" Carol turned and ran out of the room.

Now what was that all about? Jenny asked herself. She went into the bedroom and opened her closet. She *had* better start cleaning it, Jenny thought.

However, it was the end of the following week before the painter started to work on the Jason apartment, and he was just starting on the dining room on the Wednesday before the party. That day he got into an argument with Mrs. Cotton, and before the Jasons knew what had happened he had picked up his dropcloths and paint buckets and stomped off the job.

Jenny could scarcely believe it.

"Four days until my party! What'll we do now?"

"I don't know when we'll be able to get another painter," Mrs. Cotton said, "Better put everything back and let it be for now."

Jenny looked at the dining room. The walls had been steamed to remove the paper. Three of them were streaked and bare. The fourth wall—the one the painter had been working on—was painted one coat of pale green. The living room walls, Jenny knew without looking, were also stripped of paper.

What will I do now? Jenny thought wildly.

Chapter 9

Thick and Fast

Jenny sat in the chair in her bedroom that evening and thought about the words of Tweedledee in *Alice:*

> "And thick and fast they came at last,
> And more and more and more . . ."

He was referring to the oysters, of course. But he might as well have been talking about Jenny's troubles.

First there was the trouble with Carol and Grandma the day Jenny forgot to bring up the laundry. That was the day Dot said she had something to tell Jenny, "something in confidence—just between us." But Jenny never learned what Dot wanted to tell her. She had not said a word since then.

And then there was this afternoon. Jenny did not even want to think about the bare steaked walls and her party on Monday.

And now there was a new worry. Jenny could not find her library book—the book of poems by Edna St. Vincent Millay—the book into which she had slipped the letter she had written to Mrs. Fennerman. She wanted that letter back. She wanted to tear it up and throw it away. Jenny couldn't, she knew now, write to Mrs. Fennerman about Grandma in that . . . that critical way. It was too disloyal.

"Jenny!" It was Grandma's voice, and Jenny went to the door of her room.

"Jenny, come here, dear. In the dining room."

Grandma was wearing her one-piece blue coveralls that Jenny hated, but now they were a welcome sight. Grandma was dipping a fat brush into a bucket of paint, applying long strokes to the unfinished wall.

"I found some paint in the utility room," Grandma was saying, "and Mrs. Cotton said we were welcome to it." Grandma smiled. "We could get these rooms painted by Monday, Jenny."

"Oh, Grandma!" Jenny cried. "Could we?"

"We certainly can!" Grandma told her.

"And we must. I want the apartment to look presentable for me, too. Monday is my birthday."

"You're doing it for me, and you know it!" Jenny said. Grandma's birthday *was* Monday, but Grandma was not the kind of person who cared whether the apartment was painted in time for a birthday. Jenny resolved to buy a big birthday cake on Monday, with her own money. Then the celebration would be partly for Grandma, too.

"There's a lot of hard work ahead if we want to be finished in time," Grandma was saying. "Hurry now and change into painting clothes. After all," she called after the departing Jenny, "two paint brushes are better than one."

Jenny and Grandma painted all evening. They were joined by Andy and Carol and later on by Dad.

On Thursday Ruthie heard about the painting and came home with Jenny to help. By Friday it looked as if the job might possibly be completed in time for the party. Ruthie came over to help again on Friday, and this time she brought Betty with her. Carol came home early, and she painted, too.

Her mother was fine, Betty said in answer to Grandma's question. And she added with an ardor that was unlike her usual reserve, "My father thinks you are just wonderful, Mrs. Jason! And my mother, too. She can't stop talking about your kindness."

Betty turned to Jenny. "Do you know that your grandmother helped us every day—even after Mother came back to work? Mother's arm was stiff and sore and she couldn't do her usual amount of work."

Jenny looked at her grandmother. "No," Jenny said, "I didn't know it. Grandma told us that your mother was back, and I just thought she had stopped going in to help . . . I guess Grandma doesn't talk about the nice things she does for people."

"Self-praise gathers no gloss," said Grandma. "It also gets no painting done. Let's see how much we can do before . . ."

She was interrupted by Carol who observed that Pauline was late coming home from school. Andy was sent to look for his sister, but before he could leave, the front buzzer sounded. Jenny went to the door to find, of all people, Edythe Fisher.

"Your little sister is at the Essex Arms," Edythe announced abruptly, "and she is riding up and down in the elevators."

"Oh." Jenny hardly knew what to say. "Andy," Jenny called to her brother. "Andy,

Pauline is at the Essex Arms. Please go and get her."

"Is . . . is that the only reason you came?" Jenny asked. Because Edythe, having made her announcement, just stood there.

"Well . . . I thought you ought to know. My mother says she's going to call the manager if someone doesn't get that child out of there. When we chase her out of one elevator, she runs into another."

Jenny suppressed a giggle. She thought of little Pauline slipping away from Mrs. Fisher, darting into an elevator and going up, up, up—out of the reach of Edythe and her mother.

"My brother is going to bring her home now," Jenny said.

Edythe still stood in the doorway, looking beyond Jenny, as if trying to see past the foyer. Jenny wondered whether Edythe was waiting to be invited into the apartment. Jenny certainly did not care to invite Edythe in at *this* moment.

"We're . . . we're painting," Jenny said, "and everything is all torn up."

Edythe said nothing for a minute. Then she asked, "Have you seen Dot?"

"No," Jenny said. "I haven't seen her since school today."

"I've been looking for her, and she isn't any place." Edythe still made no move to leave. "Are you *sure* you haven't seen her?"

Jenny was sure, and finally Edythe turned to go.

"It's almost as if she thinks I know where Dot is and won't tell her," Jenny said to Ruth. "As if I'm hiding Dot in the cupboard or something."

Then Jenny had another thought. "I hope Dot is okay. Tomorrow is the day we give our puppet play at the Art Museum."

"We aren't likely to forget *that*, are we, Betty?" Ruth said. Betty giggled. "We've been practicing the part of the Duchess," Ruth added, "and she knows it perfectly."

Andy returned home shortly with a wailing, tear-stained Pauline.

"Gertrude and I were having so much fun riding the elevator, and then *he* had to come and drag me away."

Gertrude again! Wouldn't you know it? Jenny thought.

"We're going to have to do something about Gertrude," she said aloud. "She puts Pauline up to all these terrible things." Jenny turned to Andy. "I hope you told that Gertrude a thing or two."

"I didn't see her," Andy said. "She must have scooted when she saw me coming. She sure gets crazy ideas. Riding in elevators!"

"Gertrude gets *good* ideas," Pauline insisted.

"Where is that nice scarf you had?" Jenny asked. "Don't tell me Gertrude did away with that, too."

"I *gave* Gertrude my scarf," Pauline said. "She needed it for a doll dress."

"That does it!" Jenny said when Pauline left the room. "Monday morning I'm going to walk Pauline to school and get that scarf back. Then I'll see if the teacher can change their seats or keep them separate or something."

They all thought this was an excellent idea. Grandma thought perhaps *she* should go to the school with Pauline, but Andy said no, that would be making a big thing out of it.

"I'd rather have my sister come to school than my grandma. It's more . . . well . . . casual," Andy said.

"But it should be a bigger sister," Carol said. "If you call for Pauline before lunch," she told Jenny, "I'll meet you. I have no fifth period class, and one of the boys will drive me over."

So it was agreed that Jenny and Carol would meet in Pauline's classroom at eleven forty-five.

On Saturday morning Jenny hurried off to join her class at the Art Museum. Jenny played the Queen during the first and second acts. Jean Marie was the Queen in the last act. Betty played the role of Duchess and did not miss a line. Jenny felt that the performance of *Alice* had never gone so well. The audience applauded and applauded. Jenny noticed that Edythe and Dot did not stand together for curtain calls, although most of the principals took their bows with their understudies.

Jenny had to hurry home to get on with the painting, she told Ruth, who walked to the coatroom with her.

That afternoon Grandma and Jenny worked alone. Carol was busy with her school paper, and Andy was in a Young People's Chess Tournament at the church. Pauline had been invited to the Answering Service to spend the day there with Marge and Trudi.

"Pauline and Trudi can play until noon," Marge said, "and then I'll take them out to lunch. In the afternoon they can go to the Story Hour at the library."

It sounded like a delightful day for Pauline, and Jenny was glad that her little sister would be occupied. Jenny and Grandma could work faster alone.

It was a very satisfying afternoon. Jenny

found that she enjoyed being alone with Grandma. They worked very well together, and they found many things to talk about. Jenny discovered that Grandma, too, enjoyed poetry.

"I noticed that you had a book of poems by Edna St. Vincent Millay," Grandma said. "She has always been one of my favorites."

"I like her poem about trains," Jenny said. "Especially the part about 'There isn't a train I wouldn't take, no matter where it's going.'"

Grandma wiped her hands on a cloth. "I know exactly what she means. There's such wonderful excitement in starting out on a trip that I often feel that way, too. There isn't a train or a plane *I* wouldn't take, no matter where it's going. Edna Millay believed in being a real individual, in doing the things she wanted to do—and her poems show it," Grandma said.

"I'll bet you always did the things *you* wanted to do, Grandma," Jenny observed.

"Not always," Grandma told her. "Once I wanted to run a bicycle repair shop, but my sisters didn't like the idea at all. I guess it would have embarrassed them."

I wouldn't wonder! Jenny thought. A bicycle repair shop!

"But I did so many of the things I wanted

to do. When your grandfather lived, he wanted some of the same things—living in Europe and teaching school . . . Jenny, see if Mrs. Cotton has more of this paint. There isn't enough for the last two walls."

Mrs. Cotton did not have any more of the paint, but she urged Jenny to get some at the hardware store and charge it to the Cottons.

"Your grandmother certainly is a marvelous woman," Mrs. Cotton said. "Nothing stops her. She can find a way to do anything."

"Maybe . . ." Jenny suddenly had an urge to tease the landlady. "Maybe Grandma will go after the paint on Andy's bike."

"That might be a good idea." Mrs. Cotton laughed.

Jenny started up the stairs.

That evening she said to Carol, "Now that Grandma is painting the apartment, Mrs. Cotton doesn't even remember how she used to disapprove of the bike riding and—and just about everything Grandma did . . ."

Jenny stopped. It suddenly struck her that Mrs. Cotton was not the only one who conveniently forgot her disapproval when Grandma's activities benefited her.

But no, Jenny told herself; she really loved Grandma, and always had. And after these past few days, working and talking together,

Jenny knew that she did not disapprove of Grandma at all! She loved Grandma just exactly as she was. She wouldn't have Grandma changed for anything. Maybe Grandma was different from most grandmothers, but she was just perfect for the Jasons!

And then in a flash Jenny remembered the letter she had written to Mrs. Fennerman, the letter she had slipped into the book of poems. How could she have done such a thing? Now she wanted to tear the letter up. Jenny ran into the bedroom, but the book wasn't there. She remembered her conversation with Grandma about it just this afternoon. Could Grandma have looked through the book later and found the letter? Jenny shuddered at the thought.

"Carol," Jenny cried out in panic. "Carol, have you seen my library book?"

"You have so many library books floating around here," Carol began.

"This one is a book of poems by Edna St. Vincent Millay," Jenny explained. "And I just *must* find it, Carol. It's *terribly* important!"

"And what makes this book so terribly important?" Carol wanted to know.

Jenny was relieved from answering this by Andy, who came to tell Carol that Bunny Monroe was at the door.

Carol was gone a long time, and when she came back she said, "I . . . I guess that's the last I'll see of Bunny Monroe," and Jenny could see that her sister was close to tears.

"Why? What's the trouble between you and Bunny?" she asked.

"Everything," Carol said.

"But you used to be such good friends."

"That's just the point. As long as I spent every minute with her we were great friends. But ever since I've been feature editor of the *Black and Gold* and have to do *some* things on my own . . . Well, the minute I make any plans that don't include Bunny, she acts as if I've betrayed her."

Jenny listened to her sister's outburst in amazement. How could Carol resent a friend like Bunny—a loyal, true friend, who only wanted to be with Carol and always put her first. Why . . . why it was just the way Jenny had felt about Dot Jefferson! Jenny suddenly realized that Carol, like Dot, had grown away because of new interests. And Jenny's sympathy was all for Bunny.

"Have you thought about how poor Bunny must feel?" Jenny began. "I know what it feels like because I've been through it all—when Dot joined the Thursday Club and went to

Charm School and didn't care whether she saw me any more. I felt terrible."

"It's not the same," Carol said. "I didn't drop Bunny. I just want some time for other interests and other friends—without accounting for every minute I'm not with her. She doesn't want to be my friend, for heaven's sake! She wants to be my twin! And I don't want a twin!"

Jenny turned this idea over in her mind. Had that been part of the trouble between her and Dot? Had she wanted to be Dot's twin? Jenny didn't think so, but her sister's heated words made her see things in a new light.

"Friendship shouldn't be so possessive," Carol cried. "It should leave you free. Bunny wants to smother me with possessiveness and I told her so, and now she'll probably never talk to me again. And I don't care!"

But Jenny could tell that her sister *did* care—very much.

On Sunday Grandma and Jenny put the final touches on the painting, and Daddy helped them put the rugs down and move the furniture back. Jenny had told Carol that Monday was Grandma's birthday. Carol thought Jenny's idea—to buy a big cake for Grandma—was an excellent one, and sug-

gested that she and Andy contribute some of
the money.

"That way we can buy a bigger cake, and it
will be from all of us."

Jenny was commissioned to buy the cake on
the way home from school.

Jenny spent a good part of Sunday afternoon looking for the misplaced library book.
Finally she asked Grandma if she had seen
it.

"You mean that book of Edna Millay's
poems? Yes, indeed, I saw it. It was overdue—
so I returned it to the library."

Jenny said nothing, and Grandma added,
"Honey, I'm sorry. I should have told you
about it first. Maybe you wanted it
renewed."

"No," Jenny said quickly. "No, Grandma,
that's all right. It was . . . it was nice of you to
return it for me."

But all the while Jenny was wondering—
what if Grandma saw the letter to Mrs. Fennerman? The envelope wasn't addressed or
marked in any way; Grandma could have read
the page through before she realized it was a
letter.

All day the question went around and
around in Jenny's mind. Had Grandma read

that letter, that terrible letter that said Jenny wished she could find a way to change her grandma into a grandmother like Mrs. Fennerman?

If Grandma *had* read the letter, why hadn't she said something? Maybe because she didn't want Jenny to know how disappointed she was in her grandchild. Maybe Grandma wasn't saying anything just to spare Jenny's feelings. But what must she be thinking of Jenny?

Over and over Jenny asked herself: Had Grandma read that awful letter?

Chapter 10

Gertrude

Monday began with a light drizzle and a series of minor but annoying mishaps. Jenny broke her shoelace, and Pauline found two buttons missing from her favorite jumper. She shook her head resolutely when Jenny told her the plaid skirt was just as pretty.

"Stubborn thing," Jenny muttered as she dashed about the apartment looking for the missing pearl buttons. They were nowhere to be found.

Carol, who was finishing breakfast, offered to let Pauline wear her cameo chain.

"It will be just the thing with your nice white blouse, baby," Carol said, and Pauline brightened and allowed Carol to fasten the chain around her neck.

"Just for today," Carol said. "I used to wear

this when I was your age—but only on special occasions. And now I have to dash." Carol threw on her coat and grabbed her books. "See you at noon, Jenny."

Jenny was just finishing *her* breakfast when the telephone rang.

"It was Dr. Anderson calling from Plymouth Church," Grandma said as she came away from the phone. "They need help desperately in the church office. Work piled to the ceiling and the secretary is out sick."

Jenny laughed. "Grandma to the rescue," she said.

"I told Dr. Anderson I could only stay until three-thirty," Grandma said. "I want to be home in time to help with your party."

"There won't be much to do for the party, Grandma," Jenny told her. "The Committee will bring all the food, and the girls will help me."

"You and Pauline can have lunch at the Town Diner," Grandma said, "as a special pre-party treat. Andy is eating with Cliff Clark today."

Jenny liked this idea. It was a treat to eat out.

"I should be home by a quarter to four," Grandma said. "And if I'm a little late, Carol will be here to help you."

It wasn't until Jenny was outside that she remembered that Carol had a *Black and Gold* meeting after school. No matter, Jenny told herself. Ruthie would help her.

"Don't forget to wait for me at noon," Jenny told Pauline as she left her at her classroom door and hurried on to her own room. Ruthie was there to meet her.

"I have a favor to ask you," Ruthie began. "I want to invite Betty to the party. I know she wants to come. Miss Blake says it's okay with her, if it's all right with you."

"I'd like to have Betty come," Jenny assured her friend. "And she *is* a member of the cast. She was great as the Duchess when we gave the play at the Museum."

"I just hope she'll come," Ruthie said. "Betty is shy, and sometimes she doesn't do things she really wants to because she thinks she isn't wanted or needed."

"We could ask her to be on the Food Committee," Jenny suggested. "We really could use more help. Grandma may be late getting home."

Ruth thought this was a good idea and said she would speak to Betty at recess.

But by recess there were other problems. Jenny stayed at her desk a few extra minutes to check over her spelling paper, and when she reached the cloakroom she heard voices, Dot's and Edythe's. Jenny put on her coat and tried to slip out, but just then Dot came over to speak to her.

But before she could begin Edythe cut in, ignoring Jenny. "You promised to come to my skating party, Dot Jefferson! And you let me down now. You're not being fair."

"But I told you not to make it the same time as Jenny's party."

"It isn't my party." Jenny told them. "This is our class party—in honor of the cast and the puppet play."

"At first you said you'd come to my skating party." Edythe spoke only to Dot. "Anyway her crazy old grandmother would probably spoil everything."

"You leave my grandmother out of this, Edythe Fisher!" Jenny said, her voice trembling. "My grandmother is a marvelous woman. She has more friends than you'll ever have, because she knows how to be a good friend. And I wouldn't have a party without her!"

And having said it, Jenny realized that she meant it.

"The trouble with you, Dot Jefferson," Edythe said, continuing to ignore Jenny, "is that you're jealous. You wanted to play Alice for all three acts at the Art Museum and you were mad because I wouldn't let you."

"It was my part first," Dot said.

And then Dot linked arms with Jenny and smiled brightly. "I can't go to your ice skating party anyway, Edythe," she said, "I promised to help Jenny. She asked me to be on the Food Committee."

Jenny gasped at Dot's outright fib, but she said nothing.

"Come on, Jenny," Dot was saying now. She put on her coat and walked right by the glowering Edythe.

Ruthie and Betty were waiting for Jenny in the playground.

"Ruth says you'd like me to help with the food," Betty said. "I'd love to help—if you need me."

"Oh, Jenny has all the help she needs—now," Dot said, laughing. "She has me. She just asked me to be on the Food Committee."

Ruth glowered, and Jenny tried to find her voice . . . to say something, anything, but it was Betty who spoke first.

"Oh!" she said. "Then . . . I suppose you'll have enough help without me."

"Oh, no, Betty." Jenny was speaking at last.

"We really do want you to come, and there will be plenty to do . . ."

The ringing of the bell cut off Jenny's words. Betty waved and turned toward her own classroom.

Dot, too, ran back toward the building. Ruthie did not hesitate to show Jenny how angry she was.

"Why did you have to go and invite Dot to be on the Committee? You've spoiled everything. Betty would have come. But now she feels like a fifth wheel or something."

"But I didn't *invite* Dot," Jenny tried to explain. "She just said that. I couldn't help it!"

"You could too help it!" Ruthie's eyes were snapping. "Why didn't you speak up and say it wasn't true—that Dot wasn't asked to be on the Committee? You remember how she acted when we first started plans for the party. She wasn't asking to be on the Food Committee then."

"Yes," Jenny said. She remembered.

"Then why didn't you speak up just now?" Ruthie persisted. "Why didn't you say something? I'll tell you why," Ruthie continued when Jenny still said nothing. "You didn't say anything because you don't really care whether Betty comes or not. Sometimes I think you'd do *anything* to be Dot Jefferson's best friend again!"

"That isn't so!" Jenny had to whisper, as the girls were inside the school building now. "I do want Betty to come, and I'm going to tell her so."

Ruthie did not answer, and Jenny felt upset and troubled the rest of the morning. Ruthie was right, Jenny told herself. She should have answered Dot right there and then.

Jenny arrived at Pauline's classroom just as Carol was hurrying down the hall.

"Miss West," Carol began, "I'm Pauline's sister, and this is her other sister, Jenny. We want to talk to you about Gertrude. Do you . . . do you think you could keep Pauline and Gertrude apart . . . maybe change Pauline's seat or something?"

"You want to talk to me about whom?" Miss West continued to erase the blackboard.

"Gertrude," Carol said.

"Who?"

"The girl who is always getting Pauline in trouble," Jenny put in. She decided to try a little humor. "Who is the worst troublemaker in the whole class?"

The erasing stopped. Miss West turned to

face Jenny and Carol, and there was a wide smile on her face.

"That is a good question," she said. "We have many candidates for the post. There is no shortage of troublemakers in *this* class."

"But Gertrude must be one of the worst," Carol said. "She often puts Pauline up to things."

Miss West regarded Carol and Jenny closely. "As I said, there are several who could qualify for the post of chief troublemaker—not the least of whom is Pauline herself."

"Oh, no!" Jenny cried. "It's Gertrude who does all this. And she is always blaming Pauline and getting Pauline into trouble."

"Pauline is the one who gets Pauline into trouble," the teacher said. "And there is no child named Gertrude. Not in this class."

"No Gertrude!" Carol was plainly shocked, and Jenny added, "But there must be. This Gertrude is always . . . Well, Pauline is always getting into trouble."

"It is true enough," said Miss West, "that Pauline is always getting into trouble. Only this morning she took our two white mice out of their cage and put them in Barton's desk. When we asked her why," Miss West continued, "she said she wanted to see how they'd get along in a new environment." Miss West laughed. "Pauline has a very active imagination, as do most of the children in this class."

"I know," Carol said. "My father says any teacher with twenty kids like Pauline must have her hands full."

"Twenty-four," Miss West said. "Does Pauline often invent playmates?"

"She did make up this kangaroo with a green pocket," Jenny said, "and she used to pretend it was living in the apartment with us."

"That's true," Carol said, but she added, "Pauline has never invented a *person* before, though."

"Unfortunately," Miss West said, "Pauline does not have any girl-companions in this class. There are only three little girls in our class beside Pauline, and they are completely different from her—interested only in books and dolls. Pauline has more in common with the boys."

Carol thanked the teacher, and the two sisters said good-bye at the door. "We'll have to talk to Pauline tonight," Carol said.

Jenny pondered the subject of the nonexistent Gertrude all the way to the diner.

Pauline, who skipped along beside her, chattered gaily. It was not until after lunch, when Pauline and Jenny were walking back toward school, that the subject of Gertrude came up, and then it was Pauline who introduced it.

"I'm going to play with Gertrude after school some day," Pauline said. "She invited me over to her house."

"Now, Pauline," Jenny said gently. "You know there is no Gertrude. You made her up. She isn't real, and you know it."

"There is too a Gertrude," she said. "There is too, *is too!*"

"Miss West says there is no Gertrude," Jenny said firmly.

"She's not in my class at school. I made up that part. But there is *too* a real Gertrude."

"Why don't you admit that you made Gertrude up?" Jenny was beginning to feel irritated. "You made her up—just like Gladie the kangaroo."

"I did not," Pauline said. "Gertrude is real."

"All right, then who is she? If she is real, what is her last name? Gertrude who? Where does she live?"

But Pauline shook her head. "I won't tell you! You're too mean."

By this time Pauline had worked herself into a lively rage, and Jenny spent the next fifteen minutes trying to soothe her little sister. It wasn't until Jenny was in her classroom that she remembered about Betty.

"I didn't get a chance to talk to Betty," Jenny explained to Ruth, "but I'll try to find her right after school."

Ruth just shrugged. Obviously *she* didn't think Betty would come.

But after school Betty was nowhere to be seen. Jenny looked around as long as she could and then decided that she had better hurry home. Perhaps she could telephone Betty from there.

Jenny ran all the way home. There was no answer to her ring, and she had to use her key. Mrs. Cotton met her in the hall just as she was starting up the stairs, and handed her a note.

"Your sister Pauline left this for you," the landlady said. "I asked her to wait until you got home, but she said she had to visit a friend and you knew all about it."

The note was on yellow paper. In letters two spaces high Pauline had printed:

I AM GOING TO VISIT GERTRUDE. SHE INVITED ME. I WILL BE GONE A LONG TIME. DON'T WORRY.
                    PAULINE

Chapter 11

Pauline

Jenny stared at the paper in her hand. Where could Pauline have gone? How could she say she was going "to visit Gertrude" when she knew good and well there *was* no Gertrude?

But what if there "was too a Gertrude?" What was it Pauline had said? "She's not in my class at school. I made up that part. But there is too a real Gertrude."

If there really is a Gertrude, Jenny told herself as she stumbled up the stairs, how on earth could she be found? Oh, if only she had been more gentle with Pauline, perhaps the little girl would have told her more. Or if Jenny had come right home from school instead of waiting around to talk to Betty, she might have arrived in time to stop Pauline. Oh, if only Grandma were here—or Carol—or even Andy!

Jenny's hand shook as she unlocked the apartment door. She must do something, but what? If she went out looking for Pauline, who would be home to greet her guests? No use calling Grandma, who might be out delivering Church Tidings. Grandma thought Carol was at home, and Carol, of course, would assume that Grandma was there.

She *had* to find Pauline, Jenny told herself. But how could she walk out on her party before it even started?

Maybe someone could stay at the apartment while she went out in search of Pauline. Maybe Ruthie. Jenny flew to the telephone, dialed Ruthie's number.

Ruthie was not at home, her mother said. "Who is calling, please?"

"This is Jenny, Mrs. Kaplan."

"Oh, Jenny! Ruth's probably on her way to the party at your house. That's all she's talked about lately. No doubt she'll be there in a few minutes."

It was funny, Jenny told herself, that she and Ruthie had been trying to tell Betty Lee that she really was wanted—and needed—but couldn't convince her. And now it was true. If

Betty were here to greet the guests Jenny could go out to find Pauline.

Again Jenny turned toward the phone. She looked up "Lee" in the telephone book. There were so many of them, and Jenny could remember neither Betty's father's name nor the street on which they lived. Perhaps if she called the restaurant, they could tell her.

Certainly she could have their home phone number, Mr. Lee told Jenny. But if it was Betty she wanted, Betty was right there in the restaurant.

"I'll put her on," Mr. Lee said.

"Oh, thank you!"

Jenny explained her problem to Betty quickly.

"If you could only, only come over!" she finished in a rush.

"I can come," Betty said. "I'll be right there."

Betty must have been running all the way, because she arrived just a few minutes later, red-faced and out of breath.

"Oh, Betty!" Jenny cried as she buttoned her coat. "You'll never know how glad I am that you could come!" And then she explained about Pauline.

"Oh, she can't really be lost," Betty said. "I know you'll find her. Where are you going to look first?"

Jenny sighed. "I wish I knew," she said. "I guess I'll just run up and down the streets shouting 'Pauline!'" But even as she said it, Jenny realized that this would be foolish.

"Try the library," Betty suggested. "I saw your sister there on Saturday. She came for the Story Hour, and she was with another little girl."

"That was Marge White's little girl," Jenny said. "Marge owns the Answering Service."

"Yes, I know. Mrs. White comes into Daddy's restaurant all the time. Once in a while she has the little girl with her. Trudi, I think, is her name."

"Maybe Trudi would know where Pauline could be," Betty added.

That was an idea. Perhaps Pauline had said something to Marge's little girl about the mysterious Gertrude.

"Gee, thank you, Betty! I feel better already. You just about saved my life—or anyway the party—coming over here. And you've been here two minutes and given me two good ideas."

Jenny ran all the way to the library. Miss Kaplan said she had not seen Pauline since Saturday. She, too, thought it would be a good idea to check with Marge White.

"Pauline has been in here with Trudi a couple of times, and you may find that Trudi knows more about this than you'd suspect. That's another child with an overactive imagination."

"Thanks, Miss Kaplan," Jenny said. "I'll run upstairs to the Answering Service right now. Even if Marge doesn't know anything, we always try to tell her where we'll be. Then if another member of the family calls—to check messages—she can tell them where we are."

Miss Kaplan thought this was a good idea. "Oh, Jenny, before you go." Miss Kaplan reached into her desk drawer and pulled out a white envelope. "I've been holding this for you. It was in the book your grandmother returned for you. I guess she didn't see it stuck between the pages."

Jenny reached for the letter with a sigh of relief. That was one good thing; Grandma had not found that awful letter! Jenny took the time to tear the envelope—and the letter in-side—into little pieces and drop them into the container marked "Waste Paper" outside the building. Then she ran up the long narrow stairway.

Jenny had to wait while Marge completed a long-distance call. Then Jenny blurted out the whole sad story.

"Did you say the child's name was 'Ger-trude?' Why, that's my little girl's name. Tru-di is her nickname."

Jenny was abashed. "And all the time we've been thinking Gertrude is someone Pauline made up. A figment of her imagination, as Daddy would say."

Marge was already reaching toward the dial on her switchboard, even as she spoke.

"Mother." Marge adjusted her earphone and spoke into the mouthpiece. "Mother, is Trudi home from school? Good. Does she happen to have a little friend with her? Oh, really?" Marge laughed and turned to Jenny. "There's nothing to worry about. Pauline is with Trudi. Pick up the phone in the first office, Jenny, and you can talk to her."

Jenny wasn't sure whether it was relief or anger she was feeling when she heard Pauline's voice.

"Jenny? Jenny, there is too a Gertrude. She *is* real."

"I know she is, Pauline," Jenny told her sister. "I know it now. But how did you get way over to her house? And why didn't you wait to ask me?"

"Gertrude told me what bus to take. She told me on Saturday. She said, 'Get a Number C bus across from the library.' Gertrude is very smart. She told me where to get off. I can come home by myself."

"No!" Jenny screamed. "You stay right there, Pauline Jason. I'm coming to get you!"

"Get off at Queenston," Pauline instructed her. "And walk over one block."

Jenny, sitting at the back of the Number C bus with Pauline, suddenly felt shaky. It had been difficult to persuade her little sister to come home with her. Pauline and Trudi both insisted they had "only just started" to play.

Trudi—or Gertrude—was a bright-eyed little six-year-old with short brown hair and a mischievous grin that fitted perfectly Jenny's picture of the legendary Gertrude—the one who "put Pauline up to things."

"Gertrude is too real," Pauline said, making her point for the hundredth time. "Even if she isn't really in my class. I wish she was in my class. There's not anyone who is any fun in the class—not any girl.

"Only Gertrude wouldn't do all the bad

things I said," Pauline added. "Gertrude's not very bad at all."

"She talked you into going to her house without permission," Jenny said. "That's bad enough."

"Oh, no. That was my idea. Gertrude just told me what bus to take. And it was a *good* idea," Pauline added defiantly.

"It was *not!*" Jenny found to her horror that she was crying—right there on the bus. Why, she asked herself, was she crying *now*, now that she had found Pauline, now that it was all over?

But it really wasn't all over. Jenny pulled a crumpled handkerchief out of her pocket and continued to cry quietly into its folds. Her class party, at which she was supposed to be the hostess, was going on without her. It would be almost half over by the time she got home.

Jenny cried harder.

Chapter 12

Jenny's Friends

When Jenny finally stopped sobbing she kept her face hidden in the now soggy handkerchief. She did not want to look up and see all the passengers staring at her.

After what seemed a long time Jenny peered cautiously around the edge of the handkerchief. No one was looking at her at all. Seated in the very back of the bus, she was hidden from the view of the forward passengers. There was only one passenger in the back, and he was absorbed in his newspaper.

Jenny felt a small hand on her arm. Pauline was regarding her solemnly, with round, frightened eyes.

"I'm sorry, Jenny," Pauline whispered. "I made you lots of trouble and made you cry and everything." And then Pauline added, "Jenny, please don't tell Grandma."

"I have to, Pauline," Jenny said. "Grandma is in charge at home, and she *has* to know. Besides she probably knows already. Probably Marge has telephoned home by now and told Grandma that you were found."

Pauline looked surprised, as if she hadn't thought of this possibility. "Grandma will be angry at me," she said.

Jenny sighed. "Grandma is very understanding. But she may be upset about this, and today is her birthday . . ."

Jenny stopped. Grandma's birthday! She was to have stopped at the bakery and picked up the birthday cake. But in all the excitement of Pauline's disappearance, she had completely forgotten. And it was certainly too late to do anything about it now.

"I won't ever go away again without permission," Pauline was saying. Jenny was too miserable to answer. She pulled the bell cord for their stop. Pauline was angelic the rest of the way home.

Jenny heard her party going full swing, even before she saw it. Grandma opened the door to the apartment and threw her arms around Jenny.

"Marge called and told me what you've been through, Jen," she said. And then she turned to Pauline.

"As for you, young lady, you go to your room."

Much to Jenny's surprise, Pauline docilely obeyed—almost as if she felt that she deserved some punishment. As indeed she did.

The girls were crowding around Jenny now, saying it was wonderful that Jenny had found her sister. No one, Jenny realized in surprise, was angry with her. Everyone understood. Even Ruthie was smiling and whispering that Jenny had done a good job of making Betty feel needed.

"She *was* needed. After I called you, I was desperate," Jenny said seriously.

"I had to pick up the cookies that Grandma Fennerman put in her friend's freezer. Ours was too full to hold anything more," Ruthie said. "And then I decided to go back home and ask Grandma to come with me. All of a sudden I had this idea. I wanted her to meet your grandma."

Jenny smiled. She remembered how only last week she had desperately wanted her grandma to meet Grandma Fennerman, hoping that Grandma Jason would become more like Ruthie's grandmother. But now she

181

didn't care at all. Grandma was wonderful just the way she was. Still it was nice that the two grandmothers could get to know each other.

"Jenny, I'm sorry about today," Ruth said. "I shouldn't have been so snappish with you. I really knew you *did* want Betty to come. I guess I was just jealous of Dot for a minute. But it was really none of my business. . ."

". . . that I do anything Dot says?" Jenny finished for her. "You're right. I guess I was so used to following Dot's lead when we were best friends that I just sort of slipped back into it.

"Anyway I have other troubles now." And Jenny told Ruth about the birthday cake she forgot to buy. Ruthie was very sympathetic.

"That's a shame, Jenny," she said. "Maybe you and I can run out later and still get the cake. But now you must be starving. Come and have something to eat—if you can get through the crowd, that is."

Jenny looked around. It *was* crowded. She was sure the whole class was there, even Edythe.

"I'd better . . . well, freshen up first," Jenny said, remembering her wind-blown hair and her tears. As she made her way toward the back of the apartment Jenny caught a glimpse of her grandmother and Grandma Fennerman

182

in the kitchen, arranging cookies on trays. The two grandmothers were laughing and talking together like old friends. Jenny smiled to herself. It *was* a good party. Everyone seemed to be having fun.

Jenny was surprised to find the door to her room closed. Jenny knocked at the door, and at the same moment was conscious of low voices from within the room.

The door was opened by Bunny Monroe. Carol stood at the dresser, holding a comb. She was not combing her hair.

"I'm sorry," Jenny began. "I didn't know you had company."

"I was just leaving," Bunny said.

"Please don't leave in a huff." Carol still stood at the dresser. Her tone was pleading.

"I'm not in a huff, Carol," Bunny said, but her stiff, formal tone convinced Jenny that she was.

"I'm not in a huff at all. I simply understand that you no longer want me for your best friend."

"Oh, Bunny, please!" Carol left the mirror now and came to Bunny's side. "Please don't be like that! I *do* want you for my friend; I just don't want to be your twin—or your shadow."

"What you mean," Bunny said stiffly, "is that you don't want *me* to be *your* shadow."

What was it Jean Marie had said to Jenny? "Dot Jefferson is the kind of person who can only be friends with one person at a time." But Carol *could* be friends with many people— and Bunny didn't want to let her.

It was a funny thing. The last time Carol had quarreled with Bunny on this same subject, Jenny's sympathies had been for Bunny. Now she could understand how Carol felt.

"Please," Carol was saying. "I want to be your friend, but I want to have many other friends, too."

"I'm not stopping you."

"Oh, Bunny!" Carol sounded hurt and tired. Jenny slipped out of the room unnoticed.

Ruthie had come up behind Jenny. "Coming to the party?" she asked.

"Yes. . . I was just standing here thinking about *friends* and what odd situations you can get into because of them."

"Talking about friends," Ruth said, "have you noticed my grandma and your grandma?"

Jenny had. "They seem to be getting along well."

184

"Well, I should hope so," Ruthie said. "After all the scheming I did."

"The scheming *you* did!"

"I sat up nights trying to figure out a way to get them together," Ruthie continued. "I had what you might call ulterior motives. I wanted Grandma Fennerman to meet your grandma so she could become . . . well, more *like* your grandma."

Jenny just stared at her friend, and Ruthie went on. "It must be wonderful to have a grandmother like yours. Oh, I love *my* grandma," Ruthie hastened to add. "She's wonderful. But she's not exactly what you might call adventurous. Nothing she does is surprising."

"Oh, Ruthie! Do you mean to say that *you* plotted and planned to make *your* grandma more like *mine?*" Jenny was laughing so hard now that she could hardly talk, but she finally managed to tell Ruth the story of how *she* had worried and schemed in an effort to get her grandma to be more like Grandma Fennerman.

"It was the cookies and things she baked— and the warm kitchen—and her homey ways. I just thought it would be marvelous to have a grandma who was home all the time and baked and cooked, instead of riding off on bikes and helping people."

"Do you want to trade grandmas?" Ruth asked. Her eyes were dancing.

"No, siree! And neither do you. Maybe it's nice that we have such different grandmas. We can enjoy them both. You can have fun riding bikes with my Grandma. . ."

". . . And you can enjoy Grandma Fennerman's cooking and baking. Say, Jenny, what about coming over for dinner this Friday? I've already asked Mother, and she said she'd love to have you."

"I'd love it," Jenny said. "But I'll have to ask Gran."

The two girls were surprised to see Mr. and Mrs. Lee and one of their waiters in the kitchen. They were carrying trays and kettles of food. Betty was helping them.

"Invite your friends to stay for supper, Jenny," Betty said. "Daddy is giving a party for your grandmother."

Mr. Lee beamed. "It is her birthday," he said. He pointed to a huge cake, beautifully decorated, that said, "Happy Birthday, Mrs. Jason."

"Oh, Mr. Lee! How wonderful!" Jenny cried. Now Grandma would have her birthday cake after all. "But supper and everything!"

Jenny was amazed. "Oh, Mr. Lee, it's too mar-velous!"

"We have been planning this for weeks," Mrs. Lee told her. "Ever since I found out that your grandmother's birthday is May second. Your grandmother is a fine lady and a very good friend. And how nice it is that your friends are here today. It makes the party even gayer."

Many of the boys and girls had to go home before supper. But all of Jenny's special friends stayed: Jean Marie and Miss Blake and the two boys who played the parts of the Walrus and the Carpenter; Ruthie and her grandmother, of course, and Dot Jefferson—and much to Jenny's surprise Edythe Fisher announced that she would stay. Jenny was glad to see that Bunny Monroe, too, was going to have supper with them. A repentant Pauline had been allowed to come out of her room to join the party.

All in all there were twenty around the tables Mr. Lee set up in the dining room. Mr. Lee announced that he had invited Marge White and Miss Kaplan, as well as Dr. Anderson.

"They are special friends of your grand-mother's," he said to Jenny, "and would want to help celebrate her birthday."

All the boys and girls had been eating cake and cookies at the party, but by the time supper was served around seven, they were hungry enough to eat again. Dad came home a few minutes before seven, and he seemed surprised to see so many people and so much food.

"Is this the 'little party'?" he asked Mr. Lee.

"Your parents said they wanted to have a 'small celebration' for my mother," Mr. Jason said to Betty.

Betty giggled. "They didn't tell me one word about it," she said. "They just walked in here carrying pans of food."

Grandma—when she realized what was going on—was speechless. For once she was not ready with a scrambled quotation. She just kept saying, "For me?"

"For you," Mrs. Lee told her. "And this is only a small token of the deep affection your friends have for you."

"Your many friends," Dr. Anderson added.

The supper was delicious. There were egg rolls and soup and colorful subgum chow mein, all the things Jenny loved in a Chinese meal. And there was some American food, too.

After supper most of the boys and girls from

school had to leave. Mr. Lee would not let the two grandmothers or Mrs. Lee help with the clean-up, but insisted that his waiter had offered to stay and put everything shipshape.

"Besides, I want to have a game of chess with you before I go, Mrs. Jason.

"Your grandmother," Mr. Lee added to Jenny, "is the only person who has ever beaten me at chess."

"You ought to play chess with me, Mr. Lee," Andy said. "Sometimes I beat Grandma."

"He does," Grandma admitted.

Mr. Lee said that Andy might play the winner. He seemed glad to learn of another worthy opponent.

"Jenny!" Dad called from the foyer. "Some of your guests are leaving. They want to say good-bye to you."

Miss Blake and Jean Marie and two of the boys from school were ready to go.

"It was a lovely party," Miss Blake said, and Jean Marie told her, "It was great!"

Edythe Fisher left, too, after a brief quarrel with Dot. Edythe had wanted Dot to go with her, but Dot insisted she had "something to tell Jenny."

The "something" turned out to be an invitation to spend part of the weekend at the Jeffersons'.

"You could come home with me after school on Friday," Dot urged, "and sleep over, and we could spend all day Saturday together. I'm not going to Charm School any more," she added.

"That sounds great!" Jenny said. It was a long, long time since she and Dot had spent Saturday together. And then she remembered.

"Oh, Dot, I can't. Ruthie invited me to her house for Friday dinner, and I promised I'd go."

"You can get out of it," Dot told her.

"But I don't want to get out of it," Jenny said. "I like to go to Ruthie's—especially on Fridays."

"Please, Jenny. Please tell Ruthie you'll go there some other time and spend this weekend with me."

Jenny shook her head.

"We could be best friends again, Jenny," Dot told her. "I'm getting awfully tired of Edythe's bossy ways. And if you want to know—I think that Charm School and the Thursday Club are a big bunch of hooey."

Jenny looked at Dot in amazement. She remembered her anguish over being excluded from these activities.

"I thought the Thursday Club was so exciting," Jenny could not resist saying.

"It was fun at first," Dot said, "but how many times can you listen to lectures about the care of your skin and nails? And the exercises are goopey. Besides," Dot continued, "I miss you and all the fun we used to have together. That was what I was trying to tell you the day—when you had to rewash all that laundry. Remember?"

Jenny nodded. She remembered.

"Anyway, we can be best friends again. Wouldn't you like to be, Jenny? Best friends, I mean."

Would she like to be best friends again? Jenny thought about how she had longed to hear just those words. Best friends with Dot Jefferson!

For a moment she was tempted. It was too bad they had stopped being best friends. But then lots of wonderful and exciting things had come about that never would have happened otherwise. She had played the part of the Queen of Hearts in the marionette play—a part that was all her own, instead of being understudy to Dot. She had made friends with Ruth Kaplan, Jean Marie and Betty Lee. She remembered Carol saying to Bunny Monroe, "I don't want a shadow," and now Jenny knew that she didn't want to be a shadow.

"Don't you hear me, Jenny? I said we could be best friends again."

"Yes, I heard . . ." Jenny said. "But . . ."

"Well? Don't you want to be? The entire time I was best friends with Edythe you were trying and trying to get me to be best friends with you again. I know you were."

Jenny admitted this was true. She had been trying.

"Then why? Why don't you want to be now?"

"I don't know if I can explain," Jenny said. "But I'll try. When you and I were best friends, you had most of the ideas and we were busy doing all the things you thought of. And I didn't have time to notice any of the other kids. Then when you and Edythe became best friends, I was left on my own, and I found that I had some ideas, too. And I began to see how some of the other kids were, and they were . . . well, nice. And fun to be with."

"Oh," Dot said. "But we could still be best friends. And you could have other friends, too."

Jenny admitted that she had thought of this.

194

"But I don't know, Dot. I don't know if I want just *one* best friend again. Not for a while anyway. It's kind of fun to have *lots* of friends . . . and not have to worry about liking one best.

"I could come over to your house some *other* weekend, Dot," she added. "You and I can still be good *friends*. Even if we're not *best* friends."

"I suppose so," Dot said. But she did not sound very pleased with the idea, and Jenny felt it would not be long before Dot Jefferson found herself a new best friend. She felt a twinge of regret, but only a twinge.

When Dot left, Jenny went back to the living room and the remaining guests. The group that was left now was almost like family—Marge and Miss Kaplan and the Lees, and Betty. And of course Ruthie and Grandma Fennerman.

"Having fun, Jen?" Dad asked her.

"Oh, yes!" Jenny answered. She looked around the room at all their good friends and smiled happily.

Grandma looked up from the chess game she was playing with Mr. Lee. "Friendship is golden," she said, as though reading Jenny's mind.

"That's true, Grandma," Jenny said. "You could also say, 'Three friends are better than one.'"

Grandma moved a pawn. "Don't try to out-scramble your grandma," she said, smiling. Then she added, "The more, the friendlier."

Jenny laughed. Grandma always liked to have the last scrambled quotation.

ABOUT THE AUTHOR

SHIRLEY SIMON has been writing stories, plays and books for children for the past fifteen years, and her materials have appeared in such publications as *Jack and Jill*, *Calling All Girls*, *The Instructor*, and *The Grade Teacher*. She has written for every age child, but her favorite group is the 9-to-12-year-olds and she gathers her material from her children's friends, neighbors' children and in school yards or classrooms. "I like to slip into the back row of a fifth or sixth grade class where I am not known and just listen. Some of my best story ideas have come this way."